JATAKA TALES

ALKA

Published by :
ALKA PUBLICATIONS
2, Sai Sadan, 76/78, Mody Street, Fort, Mumbai - 400 001. India
Tel. : 2262 4439 / TeleFax : 2263 2585
Website : www.alkapublications.com
E-mail : info@alkapublications.com

JATAKA TALES

ALKA

An imprint of ALKA Publications
2006 © ALKA PUBLICATIONS MUMBAI

❀ Retold by ❀
Rashmi Jaiswal

❀ Illustrated By ❀
Vinayak Dhargalkar

❀ Processed by ❀
Meta Process

❀ Printed by ❀
Shreeji Creations

Published by :
ALKA PUBLICATIONS
2, Sai Sadan, 76/78, Mody Street, Fort, Mumbai - 400 001. India
Tel. : 2262 4439 / TeleFax : 2263 2585
Website : www.alkapublications.com
E-mail : info@alkapublications.com

Index

The Noble Elephant

*I*n ancient time, there was a dense forest adjacent to Varanasi. Once, a baby elephant was born in that forest. The infant was so cute and beautiful that all the elephants of the jungle turned up to see him. Never before, they had seen such an attractive baby. So, all of them were very elated. They celebrated the occasion with much funfare and cheer. In their jubilance they pulled down the branches of trees, uprooted many trees and small

plants. Hundreds of elephants who gathered there, trumpeted together and expressed their happiness. The occasion was a happy one for the elephants but not for the other animals of the forest. To hear such terrorizing noise, they all hid themselves wherever they could. The baby elephant who was observing everything from cheering up of elephants to terrified animals running helter-skelter, was very much upset with the whole affair. Though he was just a baby, he found the attitude of his community members very selfish. He did not like the means of celebration, which was causing so much of hardship to others. After sometime, the celebration was over and the elephants returned to their places. However, he could not forget that bitter incident. Time passed and he began growing amidst his family and other elephants. However, he never liked his friend's naughty and rampaging ways, which caused trouble and destruction for others. This child elephant was peace loving. He did not enjoy the company of his elephant friends and so he began staying aloof, away from his mischievous friends.

The elephant lived a lonely life. He wandered through the forest and roamed in his imaginary world. One day when he was sitting under a tree, he heard the crying of some animal. The elephant looked up and saw a monkey sitting alone on the tree and weeping aloud. The elephant got up and went close to him. "Why are you crying, my little friend?" asked the elephant in a very compassionate voice. While sobbing, the monkey replied, "Sir, I am ill and weak. I could not cope up with my friends while jumping from one tree to another. Therefore, my friends have left me alone and gone away. I am frightened. I may very soon be killed by some other animal."

The elephant was moved by the monkey's plight. He consoled, "Don't cry! I shall search for your friends in the jungle and soon will be back here for your rescue."

Saying so, the elephant left from there. He went ahead searching for the monkeys. The elephant finally found them playing at a place. The noble elephant went there and said "Friends, it's not right to leave your friend in distress and enjoy like this. Friends are meant for helping each other, specially when they are in trouble."

The monkeys realized their mistake. They apologized to the elephant and rushed towards their ailing friend along with the elephant. The monkey, who was ill could not believe his own eyes that an elephant who was supposed to be the biggest enemy of the monkeys had actually brought his friends for his rescue. His eyes filled with tears of joy. He thanked the elephant, "Sir, you're great! Had you not brought my friends here, I would have died." The other monkeys too thanked the noble elephant for opening their eyes. The monkeys felt that a compassionate and noble person like that elephant should be their king. So they all shouted in chorus, "Our king, the Elephant King! Long live our king."

To hear the noise, other small animals of the jungle gathered there. They were well aware of the nobility of the elephant. And when they heard about the kindness of the elephant, they too felt that the elephant was the right choice to be their king. They all chorused the song of praise for their new king whom they loved and respected so much. In this way, the noble elephant was unanimously considered their new king.

* * *

Greed is Bane

Long long ago there lived a Brahmin and his family in a small village named Chandrapur. The Brahmin's name was Girdharilal. Brahmin Girdharilal was a learned man and pious soul. Due to his simplicity and high morals, he was respected by all the villagers. Girdharilal's life was devoted to God's service. In the premises of his house, there was a small temple. Early in the morning, Pandit Girdharilal would leave his bed and begin with his daily schedule. After taking bath in cool river water, he would go to the temple and worship God. It was the bell of the temple, which awoke the villagers every morning. Hearing the bell, the people too would leave their beds and begin with their

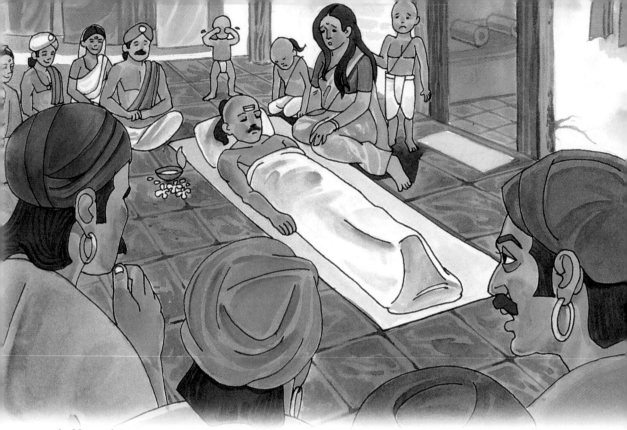

daily chores.

Pandit Girdharilal's temple was the only temple of the village. So everyday the village devotees visited the temple to pay their reverence. Depending upon their devotion and capacity, they offered God with money, milk, fruits and flowers. Though the offering was meant for God, in actual it was enjoyed by Pandit Girdharilal and his family. By the grace of temple, Panditji and his family were leading a peaceful and comfortable life. There were other Brahmins also in the village, but due to Pandit Girdharilal's simplicity, he was the most sought after during religious festivals and different rituals. So Panditji's earnings was good enough to give his family a good comfortable life.

Then one day, the life did not remain same for Pandit Girdharilal's family. That day people of the village did not awake to hear the familiar bell ringing of the temple. But they were awakened by the loud mourning voices and shrill cries. Villagers rushed to Pandit Girdharilal's house. They were shocked to find the dead body of Panditji lying on the floor. The wife of Panditji was crying bitterly over her husband's dead body. The orphaned children too were wailing with their mother. A sudden death had snatched Panditji away from his family. The villagers too plunged in deep sorrow. Panditji was loved and respected by everyone. So at this time of grief the villagers assured the aggrieved wife, "Please don't consider yourself alone. We will take care of you." Pandit Girdharilal was the sole bread winner of the family. Though the villagers ensured that Panditji's family should not starve to death, the earlier comfort and sense of security had vanished.

Pandit Giridharilalji died but not his soul. In his next birth, he was born in the form of golden swan. Surprisingly, he did not lose the memory of his earlier birth. In his present form of swan, he would often worry about the well beings of his wife and family. He would say to himself, "My family must be leading a hard and miserable life in my absence. My poor wife would be struggling in this big world to bring her small children up."

The thought perturbed him and he could not live in peace. Unable to bear more, the swan finally flew to his village to see his family. His fear was indeed true, His wife and children had reduced to a thin skeleton due to malnourishment. They were wearing rags donated by the villagers.

His heart cried to see the condition of the innocent tender children. He flew inside the house. Pandit Girdharilal's children saw the unique golden swan entering inside the house. The children were very much excited to see the amazing creature. They at once informed their mother, "Mother, mother, a unique golden swan has entered in your chamber!"

The mother rushed out of the kitchen to hear it and hurried to her chamber. She was startled to find a golden swan there. For

a few moments, she could not say anything. The golden swan said, "My dear, I am your husband. Didn't you recognize me? In my present birth I have attained golden swan's form."

The wife was still skeptical about the version. But when the golden swan told her about a few events of his last birth and about some moments which they spent together, she believed that he was indeed her husband.

The golden swan poured his heart, "I feel like crying to see my family's pathetic condition."

The wife's eyes too filled with tears. "I am really sorry, my dear," she sighed, "I could not keep our children well. What could I do without you, dear! We all are orphaned."

The wife was wailing in her misery. Tears were rolling down from the eyes of the golden swan too. He consoled, "Dear wife, please don't cry I have come back to save you from your woes. Pluck one of my golden feather from my body."

Initially, the wife was little hesitant but on insistence of the golden swan, she plucked one of the feathers. To her utter surprise, the golden feather actually turned into gold feather. She was overjoyed to see it. The swan said, "My dear, go to the market and sell this gold feather. It will fetch good money and with the money you bring food and clothes for yourself and the children."

The wife thanked the golden swan and proceeded to the market. That day, after a long time the Brahmin family had stomach full of meal and wore new clothes.

The days of misery and woes of Brahmin's family indeed became the event of past. Now it had become the practice for the golden swan to fly up to his old house and allow his wife to pluck one of his feathers.

Soon the Brahmin's widow became so rich that she bought a new big house. beautiful furnitures and different luxury articles adorned her house. The widow and children would wear expensive clothes. Everyone in the village was startled to see the overnight change in the condition of the poor widow. Everyday the magical swan flew up to the widow and allowed one of his golden feathers plucked by her and thus helped her being richer everyday. After some time she bought a bigger house and more luxuries for herself and her children. The husband in the form of swan was very-very content and happy for the transformed condition of his family.

But the same was not true with the widow. The easy riches made the woman the victim of greed. She wanted to be more and more rich and that too in a very small time. For her the swan was just a magical swan not her husband in different form. She began thinking, "One feather each will take a long time to make me richest woman of the region. However, if I pluck all the golden feathers together and sell them off in the market, I will surely become the richest person of the whole region."

The woman thought again and again on her greedy evil plan and decided to accomplish it. Next day when the noble swan came to the widow, she quickly held him with his neck. The swan was puzzled to see her behaviour. Before he could say anything, the woman began plucking feathers- one, two, three,..... The golden swan screamed to see her madness, "Stop doing this! It's not appropriate to pluck more than one feather." But where the woman had patience to hear him. She continued with her heartless work. The swan begged, "Please do mercy on me. It's causing a lot of pain and besides that I shall not be able fly if you plucked all the feathers."

Whatever the swan said to the woman, she didn't pay heed to his words and continued with her gruesome act. The widow stopped only when she had plucked all the golden feathers from the swan's body. After completing her work, she happily and hurriedly

began collecting all the feathers lying on the floor. But strange thing happened. Instead of gold feathers, there were lying ordinary white feathers! The woman began tearing apart her hair in despair to see the white feathers. She was screaming, "Where has all my fortune gone? How the gold feathers changed into white feathers?" A sad sorry voice appeared from the corner, "Your greed took away the magic and your good fortune. You were supposed to take a single feather from my body. But in your greed you didn't care for me, your husband who even in his next birth could not forget you. Now when you have chased away your good fortune with your greediness, you live in your old misery."

Saying so the poor swan hopped to a remote place. Gradually with the passing time, the new feathers covered his body. So far as the widow was concerned, she too gradually returned to her old poverty and misery. The rest of her life she spent repenting over her evil greed.

✳ ✳ ✳

The Clever Jackal

Long long ago in a dense forest, there lived a jackal couple. The jackal and his wife loved each other dearly. The jackal like a loving husband tried to fulfil his wife's every wish. One day the jackal couple returned home after a long walk of the forest. On reaching home, the jackal found that the long walk had exhausted Mrs. Jackal badly. The jackal was every much worried for her health. He went near her and asked, "My dear, it seems you are not keeping well. You look pale and weak too. Tell me what can I do for you? Shall I bring fresh meat of a wild animal?"

The wife was happy indeed to observe her husband's love and concern for her. She said "Oh honey, you love me so much. But I don't want to eat meat of any wild animal, rather I wish to eat the flesh of fresh 'Rohu' fish. I have heard that it's very nutritious and helps to regain the vitality very fast." To hear her loving request the husband jackal promptly nodded, "As you wish dear. I promise you to bring the fish today itself."

Saying so, the husband jackal left the house in search of the fish. Though the jackal made a prompt promise, he knew it very well in his heart that catching a fish was not his job and it was next to impossible for him to pick a fish from the water. The jackal was thinking hard to find a way out to fulfil his wife's wish. For long, the jackal wandered through the forest. At last he reached near a river. He knew that he was on his destination. But the question was how to get a fish. The jackal sat gloomily on the bank while

thinking over the promise done to his wife. "What will she think if I return home empty handed? Probably she will never believe my words in future and will consider me worthless," signed the jackal.

When jackal was swinging with his emotions, he heard a commotion. The jackal looked in the direction. At some distance he found two otters fighting over a big 'Rohu' fish. The jackal's eyes sparkled to see the fish. "Here's my chance!" he said to himself. The jackal promptly got up and walked casually towards the otters. The two otters had caught the fish with their joint efforts and so they were fighting over their share. The otters didn't have faith in each other when it came to the division of the fish.

The jackal heard one otter saying to another, "Though we've

hunted the fish together I don't believe you. If you'll divide, you'll certainly try to ensure a bigger share for yourself." The other otter answered, "Hold in dear friend! You are talking as if you were a saint. Dishonesty is in your mind that's why you suspect on me."

The bitter remarks, sarcasm allegations and counter allegations followed the two otters' conversation. Standing at a little distance the jackal was hearing their quarrel happily. When the two otters were firm on this conclusion that none of them could divide the fish and only a third person could do so, the jackal stepped in. In his compassionate voice, the jackal interfered, "My friends, why are you fighting over a trivial matter can I be of any help to you."

The voice soothed the fighting otters. They promptly chorused, "Yes friend, only you can help us to get the fair share of the fish.''

Pretending his nobility well, the jackal asked, "But friend, will you agree with me? After all a few minutes back I was stranger to you."

"No matter friend, we firmly believe on you. Go ahead!" said the two otters. Being assured by the otters, the jackal was all too happy to see his plan working successfully. At some distance he saw a hunter sleeping. His axe was placed by his side. The jackal went there, quietly picked up the axe and came back to the otters. He cut the fish into three pieces a tail part, a middle part and a head part. He gave the head part to one of the otters and the tail part to other otter. The two of them were very happy for the equal division. Now their eyes were on the middle. They were waiting how fairly the jackal divided the plumpest part between the two. But the jackal didn't cut the middle piece into two. He picked up the middle part and placed safely under his arm. The otters were surprised to see his act. The jackal said, "Dear friend, what makes you wonder? Is there anything in this world that is free. The middle part of the fish is my fee for the fair division of the fish pieces between you two and for clearing your fight.

Right!'' Saying so, the clever jackal walked away with the fish from there. Whereas, the otters looked foolishly at each other and their shares of fish.

They repented for not believing each other and taking their fight to a third person and thus consequently loosing the greater part of their share.

So far the jackal was concerned, he was sure that his wife would be greatly pleased that evening and their love would enhance further.

✳ ✳ ✳

The Timid Rabbit

Strong wind was blowing. It was making mysterious whistle sound in the forest. A timid rabbit was very much frightened with the whole atmosphere. He hid himself in his burrow under the mango tree.

Suddenly, he heard a heavy thud sound. The frightened rabbit sprang out of his burrow and ran through the forest. The rabbit was shouting loudly, "Run, sky is falling!"

On the way, the jackal saw the scared rabbit running. He asked, "What happened, why are you running in such a haste?" "Didn't you hear the loud heavy sound? The sky is falling. Run for your life," replied the rabbit while running.

The jackal also started running with him. On the way, they met giraffe. The giraffe enquired why they were running helter-

skelter. And when he came to know that the sky was falling, he joined them too. Soon the elephant, the deer, the horse all joined the running group.

Hearing the din, the lion came out of his den and asked, "Why are you making so much of fuss?" The animals replied in chorus, "The sky is falling down and we are running to save our lives".

The lion was very much surprised to hear this unique statement. He asked, "How did you know this?" "I saw a piece of sky falling down with a big 'thud' sound," replied the rabbit.

The Lion was skeptical about what the rabbit was saying. So he said, "Can you show me the place where the piece of sky has fallen down?"

Though the rabbit was scared, he led the lion and the other animals to the mango tree where he had heard the sound.

There, the lion saw a big mango lying. He picked up the mango and said, "So, this is the piece of sky!"

The animals were very much ashamed to realize that they ran like fools on hearsay.

The Clever Plan

Long-long ago there was a certain jungle in which there was a kingdom of birds. In this kingdom there were all kinds of birds, small as well as big. As any kingdom has its king, this kingdom of birds too had a king. The king was Hornbill. But he was not a kind and nice king. He was rather a tyrant, who punished his subjects severely on their small mistakes. The small birds were the worst sufferers of King Hornbill's atrocities. They often lost their lives in the hands of their king. The birds were angry on their king's cruelty and sad for their own plight.

So one day all the birds except King Hornbill, held a meeting to discuss about it. Each of them was sure that they wanted a change

in their leadership. "If the king is not friendly and concerned for the cause of his subjects, he must go." said the birds in chorus. After a long discussion, they reached on a conclusion that their new king should be nice and harmless for his subjects. So they all agreed to chose Bulbul as their new king. Since, Bulbul has a good appearance and is mild by nature, he was their obvious choice for the new king. However, the birds knew that without creating any reason it was difficult to remove the king, Hornbill. So all of them discussed and finally got an idea to remove Hornbill from the king's throne. The birds sent Owl to Hornbill as their messenger. Owl went to Hornbill and said, "O king, we all know that you are strong and brave. But many of us feel that a king must prove his worthiness." To hear this Hornbill asked, "What do you expect from me to prove my proficiency?" Owl replied, "O king, many of our friends think that Bulbul should be chosen as our new king."

"But the selection of king should be based on abilities rather than on the wishes of others," said Owl cleverly, "We must hold a contest to get the proof of the strength of our king."

Hornbill asked, "Which kind of contest do the birds want?" "Your Majesty, the birds want that you and Bulbul should participate in a contest. In the contest both of you will be given a branch of tree to break. Whoever accomplishes the task, will be chosen our king." Hornbill agreed.

It was the triumph of the first part of the birds' plan. The next they took the help of Woodpecker to carry out the second part of their plan. On the day of contest, all the birds gathered at one place. Owl was appointed the judge in charge of the contest. The contest was going to be held between Hornbill and Bulbul. Hornbill was called first to prove his strength. Owl pointed towards a thick branch of a tree and said to Hornbill, "If you break the

branch by landing on it with full of your might, you'll remain our king. Else you'll be removed considering not fit for the job." Hornbill agreed. He thought, "If I can't do this then no one will be able to do it, not at least Bulbul."

So Hornbill flew high up and reached at great height and then from there he swooped down with great speed and landed on the branch with high impact. But the impact had hardly any effect on the thick branch of the tree. Hornbill failed to win the contest. He sat disappointed on the nearby tree. Then came the turn of Bulbul to prove his might. The owl pointed towards another branch thicker than the earlier and asked Hornbill, "Bulbul is being given this branch as his contest hurdle. If he breaks it, he'll be considered our king." Hornbill gazed on the branch and thought, "This branch is even thicker than mine. I'm sure Bulbul will never be able to break it."

So Hornbill happily agreed and nodded for that. But here was the trap laid to defeat Hornbill. The branch, which, Bulbul was going to break, was already hollowed by the woodpecker. The solid thick looking branch was actually thin weak hollow wood pipe, which could be broken by a little impact. So according to their plan, Bulbul flew high and after reaching high up began coming down. Bulbul landed on the branch with force. Unable to sustain the impact, the branch broke. The birds cheered aloud on Bulbul's victory. "Long live our new king;" shouted the happy birds. Hornbill was ashamed of his humiliating defeat. Without saying a word, he flew away from there never to return.

✳ ✳ ✳

The Jackal & The Rats

O nce upon a time, there lived a jackal in a dense forest. His name was Chatura. One day it so happened that Chatura could not get anything to eat. He wandered in the forest with a hope to get some leftover of some other wild animal. He even tried to hunt a few small animals himself, but nothing could really work.

Whole day passed but Chatura could not get anything. The poor jackal was feeling very hungry and exhausted. So he sat under a shady tree cursing his hard luck. Suddenly he saw a herd of rats passing at some distance in a long queue. The group was being led by its king who was a big fat rat. Chatura's eyes sparkled to observe them. For a moment, he felt like leaping over them and removing his whole day's hunger. But he was clever. "I must be far sighted," he thought, "If I keep patience now, I can arrange food for next many days." So he began observing where the rats were going. Chatura saw the rats going to their burrows under a tree, at some distance away from there.

Chatura's cunning mind quickly drew a fine plan to trap them. When all the rats entered in their burrows, he went near its entrance and stood there at his one leg keeping his face towards the sun, mouth wide open and fore legs folded. Chatura looked deeply engrossed in meditation. A little after the king of the rats came out from his burrow and found a jackal at some distance from his burrow. Initially he was a little scared but when he found

Chatura least interested in him and yet busy in meditation, he went near him and asked, "Why are you standing at one leg and what are you doing here?" The jackal said, "I've abandoned the world and worldly pleasures. I devote my time worshiping sun god. My mouth is open because I take only air as my food and survive on that. The power of my penance is so great that if I put the weight of all my four legs on the earth, the earth will not be able to bear it and will collapse. So I am standing on one leg." The king rat was really impressed with this self-claimed saint. He touched his feet in reverence and the fake saint jackal blessed the rat king like any great saint. The king then called all his followers and said, "He is a great saint, get his blessings. It is our good fortune that he has come here." The rats were grateful to the jackal saint for sheltering near their homes.

One by one, the rats came and touched the jackal's feet. The rats were with full of praise and respect for the jackal who had acquired such position by refusing worldly needs. Evening set and rats took shelter in their burrows. When all the rats were gone, the fake saint, Chatura too lay under the tree to rest. Though he was hungry, he consoled himself, "Chatura, keep patience for a night! From tomorrow your problem of hunger will be solved for many days."

Next morning when the jackal heard the footsteps of the rats, he promptly got up and stood on one leg posing a saintly posture. His eyes were closed as if he was deeply engrossed in meditation. However, in reality, his one eye was half open and his whole concentration was on the rat's movements. When the rats came out of their burrows and saw the jackal still standing on one leg, they were filled with even greater reverence. Their king was the first among them to touch his feet before going on his days work. The other rats followed him. One by one the rats came, touched the feet and went away. The jackal was keenly seeing and patiently waiting for the opportunity. And when the last rat came to touch the feet, the clever jackal promptly picked him up in his paw. Without giving any time to scream, he throttled the rat and put in his mouth. None of the rats could see the evil deed of the fake saint. Chatura was indeed very happy on the success of his plan. Now it became a practice for the jackal to get his prey so easily. Far away from the tiring efforts and frequent hunger in the past, he began getting his food easily. The effect was evident. Day by day, the jackal was being fatter and the number of rats thinner. The king of the rats was wise and always concerned for the well beings of his subjects. The reduction in the number of his subjects could not remain hidden from the king's eyes. The king was worried. He looked around for the events, which were probably affecting his subjects. He observed that the Jackal who claimed himself a saint was growing fatter everyday. "How come someone surviving just on the air, grow fat?" thought the king, "Usually saints are lean and thin due to refusal to food. There must be something wrong." Once the cloud of doubt cast over the king's mind, he called a meeting of his ministers. In the meeting, he apprised them with his worry and doubt. The ministers too agreed that there was definitely a relation between the reducing number of rats and growing health of the jackal. So the king made a clever plan to catch the culprit red handed. Next day all the rats came out of their burrows in a queue and as their daily practice went to touch the jackal's feet. But this time the king was not leading his group. The king was the last in queue. When he went to touch the jackal's feet. He was careful and cautious. However, the complacent jackal hardly noticed that the king was in the end of the queue. When all the rats moved ahead, after touching the jackal's feet and the rat king came near the jackal, he pounced upon the rat to catch in his paw. Since the rat king was

cautious, he saved himself from the attack and jumped over the fake saint's neck. The truth had come out. The rat king signaled his subjects and soon all the rats who were already briefed by the king, attacked on the jackal with full force. The jackal was quite a big animal in comparison to the rats, but in front of angry and united rats, he could not do anything except screaming and that too until he could do so. Chatura got the fruit of his cunningness and fraudulence. The furious rats tore off every inch of his flesh. As a result, the jackal died a very painful death in the hands of the small rats.

The Treasure

Long-long ago, there lived a poor man who made his livelihood by selling water. Everyday he would visit the places where it was difficult to get drinking water and sold off water from the two huge pots, which he carried with him. The man's name was Bhisti. Though Bhisti worked hard whole day, he could barely manage to get two square meals everyday. Bhisti was so poor that after entire day's slogging, he could not save even a little money. But one day, he earned little more than the other days and could separate one paisa from his daily earning. Bhisti was jubilant. However, he got anxious too for its safety. Bhisti lived with his wife in a humble hut and there was no safe place in their house where he could hide the money. After much thinking, he found a place where he could keep it safely. Bhisti often visited the kingdom's fort with his pots to sell the water there. There in the northern wall of the fort, he found a brick little loose. Bhisti pulled the brick carefully, hid his one paisa in the gap and pushed the brick back in its place. The poor man was satisfied with his arrangement. "No one can guess that l've hid my treasure here," thought Bhisti with a sense of satisfaction and pride, "I can come and collect it anytime when I require it." That day Bhisti returned home a little happier than the other days. Time passed. Bhisti worked hard everyday and whenever he passed by the northern wall of the fort, he would be very pleased to feel that his treasure was hidden there.

One day when Bhisti returned home, he found his wife sitting gloomily. Bhisti went to her and asked lovingly, "What happened, my dear? Why are you looking sad?" The wife said, "O dear, I wish I could go to the city fair and could have a nice time there. I've heard that it's superb this year with so many new entertainment items. But I know, I'm not fated to see all these." Bhisti was touched by his wife's words. He said, "Don't worry my sweet heart. I've saved one paisa from my earnings and with its help we can go to the fair."

The wife was delighted to hear it. She said happily, "O really! I too have saved one paisa and these savings together will be enough to give us adequate enjoyment. Go and bring your money. Tomorrow we will go to the fair."

It was afternoon time of summer. The sun was blazing brightly, right above the head. Due to immense heat waves, most of the people chose to remain in their homes. Very few who were urgently required to go out, were out in that afternoon. The soft ground had been cracked and the cemented hard floor was working

no less than a roasting pan. But all these had hardly any meaning for Bhisti. He had to go and bring his treasure, which he saved for so long and which gave him so much happiness. He walked out of the house and rushed towards the northern wall of the fort.

Meanwhile, the king of Varanasi, Virendra Singh, who was sitting in his palace's balcony, saw Bhisti walking hastily. The king was surprised. "What made this man to come out in this blazing afternoon?", thought the king, "The man seems happy. Then what's so urgent which forced the man to come out in this hot afternoon?" The king was curious. He wanted to know the reason of his haste. So he called his men and asked them to produce the man in the court before him. The king's guards rushed and caught Bhisti on the way. "The king wants to meet you," Informed the guards. "But, I'm going for some urgent work," resisted Bhisti. He was not at all interested in meeting the king. The most important thing in his mind was to get his saved one paisa, see it and feel the pleasure. The guards were little surprised to see a man who was not bothered to meet the king. Since it was the king's order, the guards forced Bhisti to come along with him. He was brought before the king. The king asked, "O Man, what forced you to run in this hot afternoon and that too bare feet. You seem happy too. Are not these, the blazing sun and hot oven like ground affecting you? I'm curious to know the reason behind it." Bhisti bowed before the king and said, "Your Majesty, I've hid my saving in the northern wall of the fort. It's my treasure. I'm going to bring the money and the thought is giving me pleasure. Since I'm extremely happy, the blazing afternoon is not affecting me."

The king was even more surprised. He said, "Your saving must be very big for which you travelled bare feet from one end of the city to another end just to get it. Does your treasure consist of thousands of gold coins?"

"No, Your Majesty!" replied Bhisti, "It's not so big."

"Is it one thousand gold coins?" asked the king. "No, Your Honour!" replied Bhisti.

"Then it must be five hundred gold coins." said the king.

But Bhisti answered in negation. The king quoted the value of his treasure less and then lesser each time. But each time reply came negative. The king was purplexed with the continuous negative reply. So the king finally asked, "Tell me, then what's the actual amount of your treasure?"

"One paisa," replied Bhisti beaming with joy "What?" wondered the king, "Is this your treasure for which you came running to bring in this afternoon?"

The king could barely digest this fact. However, he said, "I'm really sad to see you walking in this afternoon. You still have to cover a long distance to collect your one paisa. I'm giving you one paisa and go back home."

Bhisti thanked the king for his gesture and said, "Your Honour, I'll accept your one paisa but then I'll go to bring my

money too." The king didn't want that Bhisti should measure such
long distance to collect his one paisa. So he said, "I'll give you
two paisa. Now return to your home."

"I beg your pardon, Huzoor! But I'll definitely go to bring
my money for it will add to your gifted money and enhance the
amount." Bhisti was not at all ready to budge from his way of
thinking and his words and it was making the king more eager
to dissuade Bhisti from going to collect his one paisa. So the
king kept on increasing the promised amount of gift money to
discourage Bhisti from going to the northern wall. But Bhisti was
tough nut to crack. Very politely, he refused to agree with the king
and adhered to his point. In the bargain, the king even agreed to
give one thousand of gold coins just to resist him from taking his
one paisa but Bhisti was adamant. The king was puzzled. It was
being the question of his pride. So at last, he said, "Alright, I'll
give you half of my kingdom. Will you agree now?"

Bhisti said, "Your Majesty, I accept your deal". The king was happy that he could finally win over him, even though it cost him half of his kingdom. As per the promise, Bhisti was crowned as the king of the half of the Varanasi state. After crowning ceremony, King Virendra Singh asked Bhisti, the newly crowned king, "Friend, tell me which half of the kingdom would you like to take, north half or south half of the kingdom?"

Bhisti the new king replied, "I would like to take northern half of the kingdom." Varanasi king was outwitted. He laughed sportingly and said, "You won, my friend!"

And there is no need to say that Bhisti not only got half of the kingdom but also his much precious self earned one paisa!

✳ ✳ ✳

The Jackal & The Lion

One day a hungry jackal was wandering in the forest. Unfortunately, the jackal could not get anything to eat for a long time. Hungry and disappointed he sat under a tree. Suddenly the jackal saw a lion coming towards the tree. He was scared to see the lion. He thought, "If I try to run away from here then I will be surely chased and killed by the lion." The jackal was clever. He got up promptly, walked near the lion, bowed before him and said, "Please accept my hearty respect to you. Since long I wanted to meet you, Your Majesty." The jackal's words were sounding very soft, sweet and humble. The lion was pleased to hear his nice polite words. He asked, "But why were you in search of me? Are you not afraid of me?"

"I am your subject, Your Majesty," said the jackal, "Why should a subject be scared of his king. I wanted to meet you because I wished to offer my services to you. It does not suit to a king like you to walk without any servant. I can gladly be your loyal serviceable servant."

The flattery pleased the lion and the suggestion appealed to him. He said, "You are right, dear jackal. I really need a subordinate as well as a companion like you. So from today onwards, I am appointing you as my minister."

The lion asked the jackal to come along with him. The jackal's happiness knew no bound. His wisdom assured him the companionship and protection of the king lion. He thanked the lion for his gesture and began staying with him. Wherever the lion went the jackal went too. There was always plenty of food for the

jackal. The leftover of the lion was sufficient for the jackal to fill his stomach. The lion too was happy with the arrangement for he got a companion who could give information about his prey. The two of them chose a spacious cave to stay there. Peaceful, effortless life and abundance of food with the grace of the lion, transformed the jackal into a big fat animal. Hardly he looked like a jackal. Since the jackal was the lion's associate the small animals gave respect to the jackal too and often do flattery of him. All these made the jackal very proud. In his heart, he secretly compared himself with the lion, "I'm no less than the lion. Only if I could hunt the prey on my own, I would be equal to the lion." But the jackal's craving remained buried in his heart due to a little fear and a bit of hesitation.

Where the lion and the jackal stayed, there was a valley adjacent to it. Often the herd of the elephants visited the hilly path. One day the lion said to the jackal, "Today I want to hunt an elephant. Go up on the hill and wait for the elephants' visit there. As soon as you see them you come to me and say 'King Lion, roar with all your might'. I'll understand the meaning of your said phrase, I will go and hunt the elephant."

So next day, the jackal went up on the hill and sat there waiting for the elephants. After a little time elephants appeared. As soon as the jackal saw the elephants, he rushed to the cave and said to the lion, "O King Lion, roar with all your might." Hardly the jackal had completed his words, the lion roared so loud that the animals in the forest began trembling. The lion's eyes became red and fierce. He rushed with a lightening speed and climbed the hill. By the time, the elephants had climbed down to the valley and were enjoying green leaves of the trees. The angry and agile lion standing on the hill saw the elephants and then without giving any time to escape, he leaped over the neck of an elephant. Before the elephant could understand and counter attack on the lion, his trunk was cutoff with the sharp teeth of the lion. A big fight followed. The lion clearly had a winning edge over the elephant. Soon elephant was killed. The jackal who was standing at some distance saw every thing. He was very much impressed. His mouth watered to see the thick flesh of the elephant, which the lion was eating with much relish. The jackal thought, "I wish I too could hunt the prey as the lion does. After all eating a prey hunted by ones own efforts has no match. Filling the stomach with the lion's leftover is alright but the real pride and satisfaction I can get only if I hunt it myself."

However, fantasizing to achieve something is one thing whereas actually getting that is another matter. By the time, the jackal remained busy in his fantasy, the lion ate as much as he could and then he called the jackal to feast upon the leftover.

Shelving all his fantasies, the jackal rushed to eat the elephant's flesh. He ate for long time and probably more than the lion.

Gradually it became routine for the jackal to wait for the elephants on the hill, rush and inform the lion in the cave after seeing them. Every time the lion roared hard to hear the jackal's phrase and darted out of the cave fiercely, climbed the hill and hunted the prey.

However, the jackal who went to the lion and repeated the phrase, 'Roar with all your might', began thinking that there was some magic in the phrase which changed the coolly sitting lion into a fierce, brave and agile hunter.

"If anyhow I manage these for myself, I too could hunt the mighty elephant," thought the jackal. But the jackal was scared to say this to the lion. After hiding his wish to his heart for sometime, the jackal went to the lion one day. He said, "Your Majesty, I have a request."

The lion who was living in jackal's company for long time had developed a soft corner for him. So he asked fondly, "Tell me my friend, what do you want?"

"Your Majesty, I want you to give me a chance to hunt the elephant," said the jackal sitting close to his feet.

"What? You'll kill an elephant! How can you think such stupid thing? An elephant is not small animal," shouted the lion.

"Please Your Majesty, don't say no. If you come to me and repeat the phrase, which I say in front of you, I too will become brave, fierce and agile. Then it will not be difficult to kill an elephant." insisted the jackal.

Whatever the lion said, the jackal remained adamant on his belief and words. Tired of jackal's repeated insistence, the lion agreed to do as the jackal wanted.

Next day the jackal stayed in the cave waiting for the lion

and the lion went up to the hill in search of the elephants. When the lion saw the elephants coming, he rushed to the cave where the jackal was sitting proudly like a king. The lion went near him and said, 'Roar with full might.' As soon as the jackal heard it, he jumped from his place, tried to make an angry face and fierce look, pretended to roar aloud which sounded as screaming howl to the other animals. The jackal was feeling as if he was actually the king of the forest. He rushed to the hill as fast as he could. The lion followed him. The jackal climbed on the hill and saw an elephant standing down the hill. The jackal had seen the lion attacking the elephant. So imitating him, he too thoughtlessly leaped over the hill thinking to land on the elephant's trunk. But it was not the lion who was hunting an elephant but a mere jackal. The elephant proved much smarter for the jackal. The elephant lifted the trunk suddenly and the jackal missed his landing platform and crashed to the ground. That was the end of the foolish jackal who imitated the lion without realizing his own capacity.

✳ ✳ ✳

The Little Brave Man

Long long ago in ancient India, there lived a young dwarf man named Chutku. Though his size was small, he was very intelligent and brave. The little young man was well trained in the warfare. He had mastered the art of archery. Therefore, he was an excellent archer. Chutku's arrow hardly missed the target. The people of his village and nearby villages fondly called him 'Chutku Bhaiya'. Despite all the qualities and talent Chutku possessed, his physical size was an object of ridicule for the people around him. Chutku's proficiency in archery was of no use in his humble remote village. Unfortunately, he did not know any other work to earn his livelihood. His idle sitting at home was proving him burden to his old parents. They were sad and disappointed and secretly wished if they could have a normal sized young son rather than a dwarf son of no use. Chutku was aware of their feelings and thus his own worthlessness pinched him often.

One day Chutku went to one of his close friends and poured his heart, "Friend, I'm deeply disappointed with my whole being. I'm a worthless thing and a burden on this earth. I wish to die in order to free my parents from all the troubles and pains caused by me."

Out of deep sorrow and heartburn, tears rolled on his cheeks.

The friend consoled him and said, "Chutku, my friend, please don't talk like a coward. You are a courageous wise man. Your talent may not be of any use in our small village, but I'm sure that your exceptional talent in the field of archery will certainly

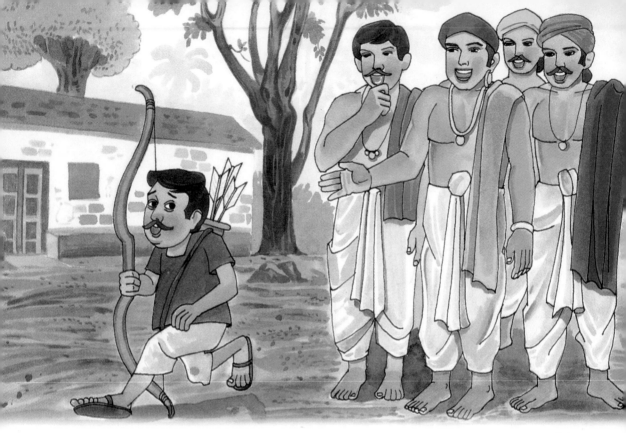

give you recognition in the king's court. Our king, Man Singh, is a great patron of brave men. He will surely take you in his shelter."

Encouraged by his friend's advice, Chutku decided to go to the king to obtain some suitable job. Next day early in the morning, Chutku went to his parents, touched their feet and asked their permission to go to the capital as per his plan. The old parents were distressed with their son's misery. They allowed their son to go away from them with heavy hearts. "Probably the fortune is waiting for my son in some distant corner." they thought in their heart.

Chutku was a sharp, able and ambitious man. But his physical size had always demoralized him in the past. Walking towards the capital, he vowed not to be discouraged by his appearance and achieve his goal. Armed with bow, he walked past several villages. But whichever lane he measured, he was looked down as an object of fun. It was no ones fault. The sight of a tiny man holding a big bow bigger than his size was in itself sufficient to thrust the giggle out. On the way people mocked, "O great archer, where are you going?"

Chutku replied humbly, "I am going to provide my services to the king. I'm a good archer."

But the people were hardly convinced with his reply. They ridiculed "Bravo! However, be careful your own shot arrow should not return to you and hurt you —— ha, ha, ha."

The similar frequent remarks were piercing him down to his heart.

"It's their fault," he thought sadly in his heart, "My size is the culprit of all the ills.''

"What if the king too considering my physical stature, did not pay heed to my words? What if the king too mocked at me and threw me out of the court," Chutku thought gloomily. In his desperation he thought, "I must engage a tall man to counter my physical shortcomings.'' The thought appealed him and he proceeded in search of a well-built tall man. While passing through a village, at one place he saw a giant like man working in a farm.

"This is the right person," Chutku said to himself. He went closer and asked, "O friend, what is your name?"

The man stared at him and replied "Bhimsen!" The man again became busy with his work. Chutku came little closer and said, "It's pity that a strong and well-built person like you is doing such insignificant work. Your kind of person should be in the king's military and should be holding some prestigious post.''

The glib talk of Chutku lit Bhimsen's eyes. He said, "But my friend, I don't know anything about weapons. This is the only work, which I know." "Don't worry my friend. What if you do not know about weapons, I'm well versed in archery and can accomplish the job of a valiant army man. My small size is the only hindrance on my path of success. You join me to compensate for my physical drawback. You'll be my outer image and I will work on your behalf. If we two work together, we can successfully secure a good position in the king's court," said Chutku.

Chutku's explanation appealed to Bhimsen. He agreed to accompany Chutku to the palace. On the way, Chutku briefed Bhimsen what he had to say in front of the king.

They both reached the palace gate. There, they were stopped by the guards. The guards were amused by their distinct pair. Bhimsen told them that he was a great archer and had come to secure a job in the king's army. He introduced Chutku as his assistant who helped him to carry the bow and arrow. Satisfied with the explanation the guards allowed them to the king. Bhimsen reached the court and bowed before King Man Singh. He expressed his earnest desire to work for the army while introducing himself as a superb archer. As Chutku had briefed Bhimsen, he introduced

him as his assistant. The king was clearly impressed with the huge size of Bhimsen. He had no doubt about his valiance considering his size. Impressed with Bhimsen, the king immediately appointed him in his army.

Bhimsen was given a big house with various other luxuries. Insignificant Chutku too began staying with him. Both were happy. But somewhere down in the heart, Bhimsen was scared. "What if the king sent him to the battleground?" - he often feared. One day proving his fear right, the king called him and said, "Bhimsen, adjacent to our kingdom there is a forest. A furious lion has rippled terror among the subjects living in the region. A big number of people have lost their lives. None of the military men or warriors, who were sent to kill him, could return alive. You are my last hope. Go and kill the lion and get my subjects rid of terror."

Bhimsen trembled to hear it but he posed calm in front of the king. He returned to his place baffled. He cursed Chutku for the entire problem. Nevertheless, Chutku remained cool to hear his complain. He said, "Bhimsen, why are you so much upset? You have to kill just a lion."

"Just a lion, Have you gone mad? I've not killed a single ant in my life and you are talking about killing a lion!" Bhimsen rebuked to hear him, "You know this very well that I don't know anything about handling arms. Even then, you are telling me to go there and kill the lion. It's very mean of you. You promised me that you'll fight on my behalf and now you want to leave me in this mess."

Chutku heard Bhimsen's complain coolly and replied, "Bhimsen, who is telling you to pick up any arm to kill the lion?"

Chutku whispered a plan in Bhimsen's ear to manage the lion's killing. Bhimsen's eyes sparkled to hear him. He thanked his friend and became busy preparing for his mission. Next day early in the morning, he proceeded for the forest. Instead of entering the forest, Bhimsen stopped in the village situated on the edge of the forest. People gathered around him to see the king's military man in their village. They bowed before him and asked the objective of his visit. Bhimsen said, "Dear villagers, our Honourable King has bestowed a responsibility on me to kill the ferocious lion which has been troubling you since long."

The villagers cheered to hear him. They were indeed terrorized by the lion's frequent ravages. Bhimsen said next, "My dear friends, I need your little co-operation. Give me a few young brave youths of your village to terrorize the lion with the noise and to help in bringing him out of his hideout. The rest will be taken care of by me."

The villagers were very happy for the fact that someone

had come to rescue them from their misery. They chorused, "We are ready to do anything for you, Sir."

In no time, around fifty young youths gathered around Bhimsen. They were brave and full of enthusiasm. What they lacked was leadership. Bhimsen posed to be a great valiant leader. Riding a tall horse, he led the cavalcade of fifty courageous youths wielding their clubs, shouting and cheering for the victory. The cavalcade entered the forest fearlessly. Nobody noticed in the commotion that Bhimsen quietly slipped out and hid himself somewhere. To hear their noise, suddenly the fierce angry lion came out of a thick bush. For a moment, the crowd was petrified to encounter their death standing in front of them. Their eyes searched for Bhimsen, their leader. But he was untraceable. The youths had no option but to fight the sudden catastrophe. With loud noise and shrill cries, all of them simultaneously attacked from all the sides on the lion. Before the lion could react, the shower of clubs threw him on the ground. The lion could not bear it and succumbed to his injuries. The victorious villagers danced in joy and cheered aloud. To hear their rejoicing Bhimsen who was sure of the lion's death, came out of his hideout and appeared before the crowd holding a thick rope in his hand. He seemed to be in great hurry. The crowd noticed Bhimsen and enquired, "Sir, where were you at the time of killing the lion?"

"What? Did you kill the lion? The king will not spare any one of you. He has particularly told me to bring the lion alive and I had gone to bring the rope to tie the lion." Bhimsen said in angry and anxious voice. All the happiness evaporated from the villager's mind. A fresh fear of probable punishment from the king, gripped them. They begged, "Sir, please save us, from this calamity."

Bhimsen posed as if he was a great saviour of them. He

said, "Considering your request I will take the responsibility of the lion's killing and save you. I'll lie to the king that the lion died in encounter with me. But remember you all must keep your mouth shut in this regard."

The villagers heaved a sigh of relief. They agreed and thanked Bhimsen for the gesture. Bhimsen was greatly happy in his heart. His mentor Chutku's advice worked. His goal was achieved without any risk and effort from him. Bhimsen carried the dead lion with him to the court. The king was jubilant and proud to see his brave soldier. He stepped down from his throne and hugged Bhimsen. The whole court congratulated him for such great victory. The king immediately bestowed numerous gifts and prizes on Bhimsen. He was given a bigger house to stay and his prestige in the eyes of the king and other people enhanced greatly.

Bhimsen was unable to keep so much joy within him. He rushed to Chutku to share. On reaching home, he told Chutku everything and thanked him for his wisdom. Both were very happy. There life had become further comfortable. Bhimsen's prestige had increased considerably. The king would remember him in every difficult time and believed that Bhimsen would be a great help.

One day a group of anxious villagers approached the court. They said to the king, "Your Majesty, a deadly wild buffalo has become a great threat for us. Every day he attacks our village and kills a couple of people. If his menace was not stopped immediately our village will be completely wiped out."

The news alarmed the king. "Who could be the most suitable person other than Bhimsen to kill the wild buffalo?" thought the king and sent his men to call Bhimsen. The great responsibility of killing the buffalo to save the villagers was bestowed on Bhimsen. Bhimsen showed great enthusiasm in front of the king and returned to his house to prepare for the next day's trip to the village. But Bhimsen had not turned into a valiant man. He was actually quivering with fear and blaming Chutku for all the trouble. He met Chutku and complained, "Hardly did I get rid of the lion and I am given the responsibility to kill the wild buffalo. In no way, I can fight with a wild buffalo."

"Who is telling you to fight with a buffalo? Did you forget the rope tactics at the time of the lion's killing?" asked Chutku. Bhimsen's eyes shone. He marveled on Chutku's wisdom and thanked him for again showing the path of rescue.

This time Bhimsen was more confident. He visited the troubled village, met the villagers, talked brave, motivated the people to fight the wild buffalo and then quietly slipped away from there. The event was repeated. When the buffalo was killed, he appeared there with thick rope and the same pretension and tactics. He befooled the gullible villagers, tied the dead buffalo and took it to the court. The people in the way shouted praise slogans on the victory. The courtiers took him in high esteem. The king was even more happy and proud for his great warrior!

This time Bhimsen was given a big palace, with many armed guards and servants, to live. He was no more an ordinary man. He had become the right hand of the king. The people bowed before him in great respect and honour. All the importance, prestige, luxuries and big palace went over Bhimsen's head. In all the hype, he forgot that all was not due to his merit but the result of borrowed wisdom. He began believing that everything, which he got, was actually earned by his own capacity. He wanted to forget Chutku, an unimpressive chap, not fit for his huge stature. He said to himself, "What did Chutku do? I too could have done that. He has not done any big job. I owe my success to myself."

This thought turned his head and he distanced himself away from Chutku. Bhimsen did not invite him to stay in his big palace. Chutku was puzzled to see the change. He tried to meet his old friend but he was deliberately ignored. Chutku could see the change but he did not want to believe it. One day he waited patiently outside the huge gate of Bhimsen's palace. When he came out sitting on a fabulous elephant, Chutku called out, "Bhimsen!" Bhimsen turned his head behind and looked at him in annoyance. He didn't like the disgraceful way in which he was called. Chutku smiled and said hastily, "Friend, why are you not talking to me now-a-days? Did you forget me, your friend, your mentor?"

"Don't talk nonsense. You are no more my friend. I am a big man now. Your company does not suit to my stature. Now onward don't try to meet me." rebuked Bhimsen.

Bhimsen asked his mahout to go ahead and moved away from there. Chutku was shocked to hear Bhimsen.

"How can anyone be so ungrateful and selfish?" Chutku's heart cried to think. But it was a fact. Chutku walked away from there sadly.

Living amidst luxuries and prestige, Bhimsen totally forgot that once he was a humble farm worker and was no brave man. However, Chutku was unable to forget Bhimsen. He tried many times to meet and talk to Bhimsen. Every time when he met Bhimsen, he was snubbed by him. Chutku was terribly unpleased by the injustice done to him. One day he went to the temple and cried there for a long time. He pleaded the God for justice.

A few days later, the king came to know that the king of a neighbouring kingdom was planning to attack on his kingdom. The king was worried for the possible mass-scale destruction. The king did not want to tread behind but he did not want any unnecessary destruction. Therefore, he sent a message to the neighbouring king to find a simple and less destructive way to finalize the winner among the two kingdoms. The neighboring king, Jarnail Singh

agreed and they formulated a way to decide the winner between the two kingdoms. It was decided that the bravest warrior of each kingdom would represent their kingdoms. They would fight each other and the winner of the respective kingdom would be considered as the victory of that kingdom over the other kingdom.

King Man Singh was very much sure that there could not be any substitute for warrior like Bhimsen in King Jarnail Singh's camp. After the important decision between the two kingdoms, King Man Singh called Bhimsen and informed him about the decision. The king said, "Bhimsen, my brave warrior, now the honour of my kingdom and my people is on your shoulder. I've full faith that you will win over our enemy. Start preparing for the scheduled date from the day itself."

Swept in pride, Bhimsen too boasted, "Your Majesty, you need not worry at all. I'll trample my enemy like an ant under my feet." The king was happy and assured of the win to hear him. He asked the treasurer to give anything, which will be asked by Bhimsen. Bhimsen did not only lie to the king but to himself too. It seemed that he did not want to face the truth in his heart. But how long could he do it. On the due date when he moved towards the battleground sitting on a grand elephant armed with bow and arrow, he was trembling in fear. A big temporary camp was stationed on both the sides of the battleground for the kings and their ministers to watch the fight.

However, there was one more person there who was scared. He was Chutku. He knew the reality of Bhimsen and thus feared the shameful defeat of his kingdom. Chutku was a brave man and a patriot. He could not tolerate the defeat of his kingdom. So he went near the camp where Bhimsen was ready to go to the battleground. Bhimsen saw Chutku. Their eyes met. Chutku said, "Bhimsen, allow me on your elephant. I'll help you to carry your arrows.''

The king who was sitting there also recognized Chutku. He liked the idea and asked Bhimsen to take Chutku along with him. Bhimsen was secretly happy. He thought, "At least I am not alone now." The elephant taking Bhimsen and Chutku moved towards the battleground. As the elephant was nearing the battleground, Bhimsen's heart began sinking gradually. He was repentant for all his boastful talks and pretension as a great warrior. Bhimsen wanted to run away from there. Chutku who could read the fear on the face of Bhimsen, asked, "What are you thinking Bhimsen?"

Bhimsen broke down, "Friend, pardon me for my past misbehaviour with you. I am regretful for all my wrong doing. Please save me, I don't want to die an early death."

Chutku was no stranger to Bhimsen's cowardice. But he said, "Bhimsen, running away from the battle ground is the most shameful and cowardice act. We must face whatever comes in our way."

Chutku conciliated him and asked mahout to move ahead to fight the enemy. However, when Bhimsen saw his opponent, he began quivering badly. The enemy warrior was no less than a giant who was wielding a grand sword and riding a tall horse. He was looking no less than the death God to Bhimsen. He begged Chutku, "Please let me go. This giant will chop off my head in just one shot. I advise you also to run away from here and save your life."

However, Chutku was not at all in agreement with Bhimsen. For him, it was much better to die for his country than to run away like a coward. He looked in pity towards Bhimsen. Chutku decided to fight alone and asked Bhimsen to go away from there. Bhimsen hurriedly jumped off the elephant and ran away from the ground as fast as he could. King Man Singh and his ministers saw Bhimsen running away. They were badly puzzled and horrified that their brave warrior was running away like a coward. "What will happen to my kingdom and its subjects?" the nervous king thought, "I staked my kingdom believing this coward." The king was shattered. Suddenly he saw a conspicuous sight. Chutku sitting on the elephant was still moving towards the battleground. "What! This little man is going to fight this decisive battle!" He sighed, "What can I do other than watching my shameful defeat." The king was sure of his defeat.

In the other side when King Jarnail Singh saw a little man coming to contest his giant warrior, he burst into roaring laughter. He pitied King Man Singh's wisdom.

But Chutku was hardly bothered about what people around him were thinking. The opponent warrior, Sher Singh saw his enemy in the middle of the battleground. He charged his horse and reached in front of Chutku's elephant. Sher Singh attacked on the elephant's trunk with his heavy sword. But the agile elephant thwarted the attack. Meanwhile, Chutku who was ready with his arrow, shot one towards the horse. The arrow went with its lighting speed and pierced the target. The horse wriggled in pain and collapsed bringing Sher Singh down on the ground. It was Chutku's first winning edge over his opponent. The people from both the sides were shocked to see this. Somewhere down in the heart, King Man Singh's dying hope began reviving.

Sher Singh was baffled to see his defeat. Wielding his sword, he angrily rushed towards Chutku to kill him. But Chutku was ready with another shot. This time his target was Sher Singh. Before Sher Singh could reach close enough, Chutku's arrow piered Sher Singh's head. The enemy roared in pain and fell on the ground. Sher Singh died in hands of non-significant but brave and patriot Chutku.

The sight was unbelievable for the people of both the kingdoms. King Man Singh and his people cheered aloud for the victory whereas Jarnail Singh and his group sank in sorrow for their humiliating defeat. King Man Singh rushed to Chutku and

hugged him passionately. "You saved the honour of the kingdom and my prestige. I am grateful to you my brave soldier. Today you proved that intelligence and skill is much important than just a huge body,'' said the elated King.

The king's voice quivered with pride and happiness. King Man Singh then enquired, "Where is that coward Bhimsen?'' Chutku told the king everything and requested him to pardon him. The king was so happy that he would have provided Chutku anything he had asked for. The king nodded to his request.

On the other side, King Jarnail Singh's sorrows knew no bound. He had lost his kingdom. He was broken. He was unable to believe that his giant Sher Singh was killed by his enemy's dwarf.

However, it was a reality. What could he do now. He slowly and gloomily walked towards Man Singh. He accepted his defeat and said, "Now I am no more a king. I am your culprit. You can do whatever you like to do with me. But I have a request. I had a desire to marry my beautiful daughter to a brave competent youth. Now when I am not a king, I request you to accept the marriage of my daughter as your responsibility."

Jarnail Singh's eyes filled with tears – the tears of repent. King Man Singh was a kind man. He said, "You are my old friend and your daughter is like my daughter. I take this responsibility."

Suddenly an idea flashed in King Man Singh's mind, He took Jarnail Singh in the side and asked, "Would you like to marry your daughter with the brave warrior, Chutku?" Jarnail Singh became very happy to hear. He said, "O friend! For a king's daughter there cannot be any groom better than a brave fearless warrior. But I feel pity that I don't have anything to give to my daughter and son-in-law as marriage gift." "Don't worry Jarnail Singh." King Man Singh consoled, "Your daughter is my daughter and you are my old friend. I am giving your kingdom to your son-in-law, Chutku and your daughter as a marriage gift from me." The people around cheered aloud, "Long live King Chutku!" Jarnail Singh was indebted to King Man Singh for his gesture. However, the brave little man, Chutku who was hearing everything said to King Jarnail Singh, "Your Majesty I am like your son. I don't want to be a king. I'll be pleased to marry your daughter and work as your commander in chief."

The people who heard it, hailed aloud for the Chutku's generosity. King Jarnail Singh's happiness knew no bound. He hugged Chutku and said, "I am proud of you my son. I would never have got a better son-in-law than you, who is so proficient and rich in qualities."

King Man Singh was very happy that due to Chutku both the old friends had become relatives. They hugged each other and congratulated. After sometime, Chutku was married to King Jarnail Singh's daughter with much fanfare. The two kingdoms celebrated the occasion together for a long time. At the end, everyone acknowledged that it was the ability and intelligence, which superseded the physical look and that the real strength lied in our minds and the skills we learn.

The Folish Tree

This is a story of a forest where there were a big number of trees, tall, huge, big and small. The dense forest was full of beasts big and small, wild and humble. All the trees and beasts lived in total harmony. The big wild animals like lion, tiger and leopards would hunt the animals like deer, goats, cow and other humble animals. The smaller wild animals like wolf, fox, hounds and jackals often lived on the leftovers of the big wild animals. The existence of forest habitat was inter dependant. It was the nature's unwritten constitution that one will provide food for the other. But in the forest there were a few trees who were not happy with the arrangement. The wild animals often left the skeleton of the killed animals or the flesh of half eaten animals, scattered in the jungle. The flesh or their parts of the animal would rot and spread unbearable stink all over the forest. The trees were dissatisfied with it. They craved to breathe in fresh air but it was not possible. One day, one of the dissatisfied trees said, "We must do something to check the filth around us. But it's possible only when these animals go away from here." A few of his friends agreed to him. But on old tree who was standing at some distance from them said, "No my dear, never think like this. Though we need fresh air to breathe, we must not forget that these animals are necessary for our survival. They are our patrons. A forest without animals could well be cleaned by the human beings anytime."

However, the angry young trees could not realise the gravity of the old tree's words. Without paying heed to his advice, they were determined to chase the animals from the forest. And then one day they got a chance to do so. One night the wild animals were sleeping under these trees and a pleasant breeze was blowing. The trees who were in search of an opportunity, signaled each other. Determined to scare the wild animals, they began swaying with all their might. The trees were making mysterious and terrifying sounds. The strange sound and sudden hard wind blow indeed horrified the animals. They perceived that the place was haunted so without thinking much, all of them ran away from there never to return again. The animals were gone and the young trees were jubilant on the success of their plan. However, the development made the old tree worried. Since the animals had gone, there were no more rotten flesh, bare skeleton and poisonous stink. The air in the forest was fresh and filled with fragrance of the wild flowers. The trees were happy and feeling good.

Some time passed. One day a cowherd boy of adjacent village entered the forest, chasing his calf. Though the boy entered in, he was apprehensive about the probable wild animal's attack. Calling the name of his calf, he cautiously moved in. But surprisingly enough the forest was totally quiet, without the feeblest sound of any wild animal. The boy did not see a single animal inside the forest. After a while the boy found his calf and taking it, he returned to the village. As soon as he reached, he informed his father that the adjacent forest was without any animal. The father

was very much surprised to hear it. Next morning he himself visited the forest and found the truth in the words of his son. He then happily returned to the village and informed about it to the other villagers. In no time, a big number of villagers with their axes and ropes reached the forest. They said to each other, "If we cut these trees, we can use this place for farming." Saying so they began cutting the trees. The poor trees began falling to the ground in no time. The young trees who had scared the beasts away from the forest said to each other, "We must frighten these men also."

With this, they began blowing hard. But the men were not scared. However hard they blew and produced mysterious sound, the men were hardly deterred. Now it was time for the young trees to be frightened. The old tree who was observing everything said, "My friends, once I warned you against staying without the wild animals. But you didn't listen to me. See its consequences and face it."

The young trees were ashamed for not obeying the advice of his elder. But repenting over uncorrectable act is of no use. They were seeing their death coming closer to them every moment. Very soon, the villagers cut off all the tree of the jungle including those young trees and used the place for farming.

The Gardener & His Monkey Friends

The king of Varanasi was very much fond of greenery and flowers. A beautiful garden with a variety of flowers and rare plants was cultivated at some distance from his palace to suit his liking. An adroit gardener looked after the plants and maintained these beautifully.

Once it so happened that the religious festival, 'Maha Kumbh' was round the corner. Everyone from the king and his family to his subjects were supposed to visit the town, where it was going to be celebrated. The royal gardener, too desired to attend the festival, but he knew it was not possible. The gardener thought sadly, "I wish, I too could visit the festival. But then who will water these plants and look after the needs of these plants?"

The thought made him disappointed and gloomy.

At some distance from there, lived a group of monkeys who often visited the royal garden. The chief of the monkeys had become a good friend of the royal gardener.

That day when the gardener was sitting gloomily, the chief of the monkeys visited the garden. "You are looking anxious friend, what's the reason?" asked the chief.

"From tomorrow the festival of Maha Kumbh is going to start. I had a long crave to visit the festival for it comes after the period of twelve years. But I know I shall not be able to attend." replied the gardener.

"But why can't you?" asked the chief. "My job will not allow me to move from here even for a single day, whereas to attend the festival I shall have to go away from here at least for five days. In between the plants and flowers of the garden will dry up without water," sighed the gardener.

"That's all the cause of your worry?" said the chief, "Then forget about your disappointment. Go and get ready to attend the festival. Meanwhile, my companions will look after the garden and its plants very well."

The gardener was pleasantly surprised to hear this, "Are you sure that they can accomplish this job?"

"Of course! We shall certainly take a good care of these plants." assured the chief.

The gardener was quite relieved to hear this. He thanked the monkey chief and went away from there to attend the festival.

The chief then called his companions. Soon all the monkeys gathered there. "There is a very important task for all of us to perform. Till our gardener friend comes back from the town, we have to take a very good care of this royal garden," informed the chief.

The monkeys cheered aloud to hear this, "It will be indeed a great fun for us." They all rushed to collect the buckets and other pots and filled those with the water. After filling the buckets, they rushed to the plants. But the monkeys were little puzzled for the plants were of different sizes. They were not sure that what amount of water they should pour in each plant. The monkeys called their chief who was the most intelligent among them and asked, "Chief, we are a bit confused. Help us to ascertain the exact amount of water required for each plant."

Hearing them and having a closer look at the plants the chief remarked, "It's not so difficult. Before watering any plant, you uproot it and then see the size of the roots. If the roots are bigger and thicker, it means the plant requires more water. If the roots of any plant is less developed this shows the plant will do with less water. Isn't it quite simple?"

The chief was boastful for his own knowledge and his companion was proud about it.

The enthusiastic monkeys began uprooting the trees and plants before watering them. So was their zest that in the next three days all the plants of the garden were uprooted.

After five days of excursion, the gardener returned to the city. After reaching the city, he at once set out for the garden. "Hope, my monkey friends would have taken a good care of the royal garden," thought the gardener as he was on the way to the garden.

But when he reached there he was terribly shocked to

witness the unimaginable devastation. All the big and small trees and plants had been uprooted. All of them had dried. His years of skill and honest labour had gone in vain. The whole garden was ruined.

The gardener trembled to see it and sat down on the ground holding his head in his hands. " What will I answer to the king?" he sighed. "I got the right punishment for depending upon foolish well wishers," the gardener cursed himself repenting for his folly.

* * *

The Jackal &
The Goat

*I*n the mountains of Himalayas, there lived a big family of goats. The goat family loved each other very much and they lived with great unity. Whole day the goat would graze in the sprawling green meadow of the mountain valley and by the evening, they returned to their cave. The goat family was very happy and in peace, till a jackal couple had not noticed them and their mouth had not watered to see the tender goat kids.

One fateful day when the herd of goat family was returning in the evening to their cave, a greedy cunning jackal couple happened to pass by the way.

"What a fine plump kids are these." the husband sighed to observe the kids who had strayed away from their herd and were playing on the hills, "These little things will certainly give a great amount of pleasure. Let's plan carefully to pick a goat everyday and enjoy our life."

The wife admired the cunningness of her husband, "Fabulous! Your idea is perfect. We must find a place to stay somewhere nearby to the goat's shelter and then we can relish them without much effort."

The jackal couple found out an empty cave and began staying there. Every evening the herd of goats passed through the mountain's way. The jackal couple hiding amidst the hill would quietly pick up a kid, took it into their cave and ate happily. Initially, the goat didn't sense danger about the missing kids. They thought, "Probably, the naughty playful kids have strayed away amidst the hills." But the decreasing number of the goats pressed the alarm bell in their mind. They guessed that some of their enemy was picking away their children. However, the jackal was much shrewd to tackle the wisdom of the goats. Despite the increased carefulness of the goats, the jackal couple continued to succeed in their nasty act. The goat family was greatly worried for their waning number. The simple goats didn't know how to protect themselves. If the goats didn't visit the meadow they would surely die of hunger. Many times, they had seen the jackal couple roaming and had guessed that they were their actual enemies. However, the number of goats continued diminishing. And one day barring a senior most female goat whose name was Rani, each one was killed and eaten by the jackal. Rani, could not become the prey of the jackals due to her wisdom and extreme alertness. However, Rani was very sad and alone. She was full of anger and hatred for the jackal couple who had wiped her entire family. But then she was scared for her life too. She stopped visiting meadow to graze for the fear of her life. Rani would come out of her cave for very little time to collect some green grasses and leaves to feed herself. Her fear had virtually imprisoned her in her cave.

The jackal couple were finding it extremely difficult to get Rani. In the past they got and killed any of the goats whom they liked. But Rani was too clever to be their prey. As the days advanced, the desperation of husband jackal to kill Rani increased. His sly mind was thinking to find a way out to grab Rani. And then one day a nasty shrewd idea sprouted in the husband Jackal's mind. He asked his wife to go to Rani and befriend her with various lies and pretension. The wife appreciated her husband's plan. After being briefed by her husband, she moved towards Rani's cave. Standing outside the cave, the wife of the jackal called out, "O friend goat, can

you hear me? I'm here to do friendship with you. Please come out."

Rani heard the calling and peeped out, "She is the wife of cruel jackal," thought the goat, "I must not believe her."

"Go away!" Rani sceamed in anger, "You are a murderer. You killed all my near and dear ones and forced me to live alone in this world."

"I know you are alone and so I'm." replied the she jackal, " But believe me, I'm in no way involved in all the wrong doings of my husband. He is a sinner and because of all his misdeeds nobody wants to be my friend." Saying so the jackal's wife began to cry. Rani was kind hearted. Though she was apprehensive, she could not see her crying. "I want to believe you but because of your husband. I can't do so." said Rani.

The she jackal wiped her eyes and said, "I can understand all your apprehension and feel sorry for your plight. If you can't come out, don't do so. But please don't refuse to talk to me." The goat agreed. "I am alone too," thought Rani, "There is nothing wrong in talking from inside." So goat and the wife of jackal became friends. Initially, Rani was cautious and didn't allow the she jackal inside her cave or went near her. However, as the time passed, she was relaxed and less cautious. Rani began considering Mrs. Jackal as her friend. They often spent long hours chatting with each other. Then one day when Mrs. Jackal felt that she had won Rani's trust fully, she decided to carry out her further plan. She went to meet Rani. Her eyes were wet. "What happened?", asked Rani. "Today my husband died." replied the wife, "No doubt he was a cruel person. But he was my husband. I'll have to perform his last rites and bury him in the ground. Please help me to do so." The she jackal was sobbing. "No, no, I can't help you. I hate him and I am scared of him too," replied the goat instantly. "You are right my friend. Who would like to stand by the side of a sinner's widow." said the she jackal, "I knew I'm alone in this world but yet I hoped that my dear friend Rani would certainly come for my help at this hour of grief." Saying so she began crying bitterly. The treacherous she jackal pretended so well that Rani felt really sorry for her plight and decided to help her. Mrs. Jackal was rejoiced to trap Rani in her web. Rani came out of her cave and accompanied the she jackal to go to the place where her dead husband was lying. But somewhere down the heart, Rani was still apprehensive and so cautious. She asked the she jackal to move ahead showing her the path and Rani remained little behind just to keep herself at a safe distance.

Meanwhile, the jackal who was lying pretending dead, heard

the footsteps. He considered that close enough to attack. In his desperation to see his prey, he opened his eyes a little to see. But what he didn't know was that, wise Rani was careful. She saw him opening his eyes and immediately fled away and reached her cave to her safety. Rani was very-very angry and annoyed at the she jackal's treachery. Whereas she jackal was terribly disappointed and angry with her husband due to his foolishness. "You spoilt everything." she rumbled, "I won her trust with so much effort and you allowed the golden opportunity pass due to your impatience." The husband jackal was regretful and sad for his stupidity. "I am sorry!" said the jackal to his wife, "I am really a fool, but give me a chance. This time I won't disappoint you. Bring her here anyhow."

"Alright! I'll go and try again," assured the wife. The jackal's wife went again near the goat's cave and called out, "Sister goat, You proved to be a prophet for me. Mere your presence gave life to my dead husband. He is extremely grateful to you and wants to meet you. I've come here to invite you for a feast on this happy occasion." Rani was well aware of she jackal's treachery and pretension. She thought, "This sly jackal considers me so gullible that she expects me to believe her words even now. All right! Now I must give her a befitting reply." Rani didn't show any anger, rather she said in a very sweet voice, "O really my friend! I am very happy that your husband is alive. I'll certainly attend your feast. But you know I am scared from your husband due to past unfortunate reasons and so I would come to your place with some of my friends."

" Who are they?" asked the she jackal.

"They are hounds. They are just two thousand in number. Now go and do arrangements for our feast. We are coming soon." said Rani. "Hounds—— two thousand hounds!" blurted she jackal. She was badly frightened to think about the probable dangerous

guests at her place. She said, "My friend, since you are scared of my husband. I don't force you to come."

"But I would like to attend your feast with my friends," said the goat beaming with joy to see the blanched face of she jackal. However, Mrs. Jackal didn't say anything except running away from there as fast as she could. She stopped only when she reached at her place. "Hurry up! Two thousand hounds are coming to attend our feast. We must run away from here before they actually arrive here. The goat proved much smarter than us." Saying so the she jackal began running. The jackal too followed her in fright. The cunning jackals ran away from there never to return again. The wise goat saved her life with her wisdom and lived a peaceful life thereafter.

✳ ✳ ✳

Friends in Need

Once upon a time, there lived four friends - a deer, a mouse, a crow and a tortoise. The mouse lived in a hole beneath a Banyan tree. The deer lived under the same shady Banyan tree. The crow lived on a branch of the Banyan tree and the tortoise lived in a nearby lake.

All were good friends. Everyday they all gathered under the tree, talked to each other and enjoyed their lives together.

One day the deer went to graze in the deep forest and did not come back till late in the evening. The worried mouse asked the crow, "It seems our friend is in some trouble. Please go flying and search him out."

The crow too was anxious for his friend. He immediately

flew in search of the deer. Soon, he found the deer in the hunter's trap. The deer was unsuccessfully trying to come out of the net. However, the hunter was not visible there. So the crow came down and sat near the deer. The deer's eyes twinkled to see his friend.

The crow said, "I'm extremely sorry to see you in this trouble. Don't worry. I'll do something to free you from here. First tell me where is the hunter?"

The troubled deer replied, "He has gone to bring the rope to tie me."

The crow consoled him and said, "Maintain your calm. Soon I'll be back to you with our friend mouse."

The crow flew back to the Banyan tree as fast as he could. He quickly informed the mouse about the mishap. The crow asked the mouse to ride over his back. Then the crow quickly flew towards his friend deer. On the way they met their fourth friend, the tortoise.

When the tortoise saw both of them rushing, he anxiously asked the whereabouts of the lost deer. But the crow was in hurry. So he said in brief, "The deer is in the hunters net. I'll tell you the details after coming back from there."

The reply made the tortoise more anxious and worried. He too proceeded in the same direction at his slow pace. When the crow reached up to the deer, the hunter was yet to come back. The mouse climbed down from the back of the crow and swiftly nibbled the net. The deer was free then. He thanked his friends. By that time, tortoise also reached there. He was happy to see the deer out of the danger.

Suddenly they saw the hunter coming back. They said to each other, "Let's run fast."

With this they all escaped swiftly except for the poor tortoise.

The tortoise tried hard to run, but he could not. When the hunter saw his prey going out of his clutch he shouted. However it was not so easy to chase a deer.

Suddenly he noticed the tortoise crawling on the ground. The hunter picked him up and roped him to his hunting stick. While flying, the crow looked down. He was shocked to see his friend tortoise tied with the hunter's stick. All the happiness vanished.

The remaining three friends again gathered. They discussed how to save their friend tortoise. After chalking out their plan, they all reached near the hunter's house.

When hunter reached his house, he saw the deer standing there. Happy hunter chased the deer again.

The deer ran away swiftly. But he kept on giving his glimpses to the hunter just to elude him. The crow was following the hunter through the sky, while the mouse was running after the hunter on the ground.

After running for sometime, the hunter found it difficult to run along with his bag and stick. So he dropped his bag and stick on the ground and then chased the deer fast. When the deer saw the hunter leaving his stick on the ground, he ran faster than before. Soon the deer drove the hunter far away from there. When the crow saw the stick on which the tortoise was tying, he swooped down and called the mouse. The mouse started his work again, however the crow flew to the sky to keep a watchful eye for the hunter.

The mouse cut the rope efficiently and freed the tortoise. Tortoise immediately slipped into the thick bushes. The mouse continued on his path. The crow flew fast and indicated the deer that the work was accomplished. Then the deer ran with a lightening speed and vanished in a trice.

The hunter returned empty handed. He consoled himself, "At least I've tortoise with me for today's meal."

But when he reached the place where he had left the stick and bag, he found the rope nibbled.

He was shocked and felt sorry to run after the uncertain, leaving behind his certain gain.

And all the four friends lived happily ever after.

A Lesson to the Elephant

A sparrow couple lived on a branch of a blackberry tree. The couple had a comfortable nest where they lived happily. After some time, the female sparrow laid eggs. The couple was happy. They were waiting for the arrival of their children very eagerly.

One-day, a mighty elephant came wandering near the blackberry tree. The elephant liked the leaves of the blackberry tree. So he lifted his trunk above to pull down a branch of the tree. The sparrows saw the elephant, who was about to pull the branch. They screamed, "O mighty elephant! Please don't pull the branch. Our nest is built on this tree and there are eggs in the nest. We are anxiously waiting for our babies to come out. If you disturb

this tree then our nest will fall down destroying the eggs."

The arrogant elephant did not pay any heed to the birds. He pulled down a big branch, which resulted in shaking of the whole tree vigorously. As apprehended, the nest came down and all the eggs were broken. The couple cried bitterly. The callous elephant enjoyed the leaves and went away from there peacefully.

The sparrow couple was angry and revengeful. The couple went to seek help from their other tiny friends. The crow couple, the frog, the gnat and many other friends consoled the sparrow couple. All of them sat together and made a plan to teach the elephant a lesson.

Next day when the elephant came wandering, the gnat efficiently entered into the elephant's ear and started droning. Continuous droning in the ear by the gnat made the elephant dizzy. He fell down. Now it was the turn of the crow couple to attack. The crow couple who were sitting on the tree, swooped down fast and pecked in elephant's both the eyes with their sharp

beaks making him blind. The elephant cried aloud in pain.

The elephant was totally baffled by these sudden attacks. The wounded elephant's throat and mouth were parching. So he ran towards the lake with his blind eyes. Now it was the turn of the frog. The frog jumped into a huge ditch and started croaking aloud. Hearing the frog's croak, the blind elephant thought that he was close to the lake and ran in the direction of the ditch which led him inside the ditch. The arrogant elephant died a miserable death.

* * *

Pandit Aushadha Kumar

Long long ago, an infant was born in the family of Mithila Kingdom's resident. The strange thing was that the boy appeared in the world clinching a divine herb in his fist. Since the herb was rare and possessed excellent healing power, he was named Aushadha Kumar.

Before Aushadha Kumar's birth, one day the king of Mithila, Mithilesh had a wonder dream. In his dream, he saw that a child of exceptional merit was very soon going to take birth in his kingdom. He heard a divine prediction that the child will be unique considering his wisdom and talents. King Mithilesh awoke wondering over such strange dream. The king was sure that it was a divine message. A few months later the child, Aushadha Kumar was born. The king remained ignorant about it. Meanwhile the child, Aushadha Kumar began growing. The people around him often witnessed the different shades of child Aushadha Kumar's intelligence.

When Aushadha Kumar was around eight years, Mithila King came to know about this bright child. The child reminded him of his dream. The king was very much sure that he was a great soul. So the king adopted Aushadha kumar and brought him to the palace. Aushadha Kumar began living under King Mithilesh's guardianship. With the time, Aushadha Kumar grew up in a fine youth. He always accompanied the king, be it the court or somewhere else. Aushadha Kumar's intelligence and humility had made him the apple of the king's eye. The king took his advice on every important matter and worked as per his suggestions. But not everyone in the court was happy with Aushadha Kumar's ability and the importance, which he was deriving from King Mithilesh. A few senior courtiers, who were enjoying the king's grace and patronage before Aushadha Kumar's inclusion in the court, were disappointed and envious due to their reduced importance. Pandit Dwivedi was one among the jealous courtiers.

One morning a few people saw a beautiful sparkling gem inside the city water tank. Since the gem looked quite precious, they dived inside the tank to get it. However, the tank was deep and they could reach its floor to get it. They tried several times but could not succeed. Later on, they decided to inform about the gem to the king. The king with his prominent courtiers arrived the spot to view the gem. The gem yet looked precious. The king ordered the best diver of the city to fetch the stone. The diver tried, but failed to reach the bottom thus did not succeed in bringing the stone.

Pandit Dwivedi who had come with the king thought, "Before Aushadha Kumar finds any way to obtain the gem, I must do something to get it and impress the king." So Pandit Dwivedi promptly called the incharge of the tank and asked him to empty the tank. Aushadha Kumar who was standing there tried to stop him from doing so and said, "Please wait, it will not help you to get the gem."

Before he could say further, he was interrupted by the agitated Pandit, "Let me do my work. I have taken the responsibility and I know how to do it." To hear Pandit's snubbing, Aushadha Kumar remained quiet. The tank was emptied. The people around were eagerly waiting to see the big precious stone. The king too was curious. As soon as the tank was emptied the gem disappeared leaving the people wonder struck and puzzled. Pandit Dwivedi asked the tank incharge to fill the tank. No sooner did the water was filled in the tank that the gem appeared from nowhere.The people were even more puzzled and confused, but not Aushadha Kumar.

He came forward and said to the king, "Your Majesty, the gem is not in the tank." "Then where is it?" was the spontaneous question from the king. Aushadha Kumar managed to bring a deep platter, filled it with water and kept near the tank. This time the gem could be seen into the platter. The people were startled. Aushadha Kumar said, "The gem is neither inside the tank nor in the plate. It's just the reflection of the precious gem which in somewhere nearby." After observing the light's direction, which had been reflecting the stone inside the tank or the platter, Aushadha Kumar concluded, "The stone is in the crow's nest, which is built on a tall palm tree, standing a little distance away from there." Immediately the king's men climbed the palm tree. The gem was indeed found in the nest. The stone was really big and invaluable. The king was overjoyed to see it. He patted Aushadha Kumar's back and praised high for his wisdom. Pandit Dwivedi once more failed to please the king and that annoyed him even further.

Meanwhile an important event happened which influenced the king's life later on.

In the Kingdom of Mithila, there was one Gurukul, amidst the forest. It was the tradition of that Gurukul that the senior most pupil married the eligible daughter of the Gurukul's Acharya (teacher). So one day when the senior most student of the Gurukul completed his studies and sought the permission to go away from there, the Acharya said, "My dear, according to tradition, you will wed my young daughter and make her your wife." The young man was hesitant. He tried to resist but the Acharya refused to listen. The young man was married to the Acharya's daughter. The girl was exceptionally beautiful and was well talented in many faculties. The young man was well aware of all her qualities. So he was feeling himself insignificant in front of her and that was giving him an uneasy feeling. Though he could not say anything to Acharya and as per his command, set out along with his newly wed wife, he was anxious and was thinking hard to get rid of her. As the couple was passing through the forest, they came across a goollar tree (a wild fruit bearing tree). To eat a few, the young man climbed the tree. After reaching at comfortable place, he' plucked a few and began eating. The wife who was standing down, was hungry. She too felt like eating the fruits. So she requested, "Please throw a few for me too."

"Climb on the tree and get it yourself," replied the husband rudely. The poor wife had no other option than to climb the tree herself. With great difficulty she reached the height from where she could pluck the fruit. As soon as she reached up, the young man climbed down fast. He found it the right opportunity to get rid of the woman. The woman was shocked to see him going away from there. She called out anxiously, "Where are going?"

"Away from you," said the young man shamelessly, "I had been forced to marry you and this is the only remedy I see for

all my troubles." Saying so, the man ran away from there leaving his wife stranded on the tree. The poor girl screamed to stop him but in vain. The man didn't stop to hear her cries.

Two days later King Mithilesh passed through the same forest with his cavalcade. At one place, he found a beautiful woman sitting amidst the branches of a tree. She was looking pale and tired. The king was curious. He asked his minister to enquire the reason for sitting at such an odd place. The minister went to the woman and asked the reason. The woman told the tale of her plight. The minister returned and narrated everything to the king. The king felt sorry to hear her tale. "The man must be unfortunate and worthless who abandoned such beautiful wife," the king thought. He discussed the matter with his advisors. Since it was the duty of a king to protect his subjects, it was advised to take the woman to the palace. So young woman also accompanied the king's cavalcade. On reaching the palace, the woman was sent to the guest palace. The king too returned to his palace. But the king was still thinking about the woman. Her lovely cool face was frequently appearing in his mind. He was unable to forget her. Her look and manners were fit to be a queen. The king spent whole night thinking about her. Next morning he called the royal priest and sought his advice in this matter. The royal priest said, "O king, if a woman is abandoned by her husband and if there is no one to take care of her, it's the king's responsibility to provide her shelter. And what can be a better way to do so if the king accepts her as his wife?"

After getting nod from the royal priest, the king met the woman, expressed his wish to marry her and sought her wish in the matter. The woman happily agreed and said, "I'll be the most fortunate woman to be your wife." The woman was married to the king. She indeed proved a caring wife and fair queen. The king was happy to get such wife and the couple spent nice time with each other.

One day King Mithilesh and his queen were enjoying the boat ride in River Ganga. Suddenly the queen's eyes fell on a group of labourers who were working on the bank. One of the labourers looked familiar to her. She watched him keenly and remembered that it was none other than her previous husband who ran away leaving her stranded on the tree. Instantly, the queen's face lit with a smile to see the destiny's changed face. "He abandoned me to face the crisis, but see where he is and where I am?" thought the queen. Suddenly the king saw the queen smiling at a man, working on the bank and fumed. He considered her act not suitable to his wife and asked the queen angrily, "What made you smile to see the man?"

The queen was shocked to hear his question. She replied, "My lord, he is my former husband and I smiled because…." The king who had lost his temper and hardly had patience to hear

her explanation, interrupted in between, "Oh! That is the reason why you smiled! This shows you have still a soft corner for that treacherous man."

"No, Your Majesty! It's not right!" the queen begged.

The angry king was not ready to listen to the queen. "You are a liar and deceiver. You still love him. You must get punishment for your crime," commanded the king, "You must be hanged for your severe folly." The queen wept to hear it. She pleaded the king to believe her but the king didn't soften. At last, the queen said, "O my Lord, please don't take such grave decision in haste. Take the advice of your wise courtiers." The king agreed. On reaching the palace, he called Pandit Dwivedi and Pandit Aushadha Kumar. He told them about the incident and asked, "What do you think about it?"

Pandit Dwivedi was always in search of an opportunity to please the king. So instead of speaking his heart, he decided to nod with the king to access his favour. "A woman's character is always doubtful. This truth has been repeatedly mentioned in our epics and verses," said Dwivedi cunningly, "I beg your pardon Huzoor, the queen may not be the exception of such popular belief."

The king then asked the view of Aushadha Kumar. "Your Majesty, I disagree with respected Panditji. The reason of her smile lies somewhere else. It's the indication of her happiness, which the destiny and the twist in events gave her. She must have smiled to see the irony. The man who left her was leading a miserable life. Had he not left her, she too would be living an ordinary life with full of woes. But the abandonment proved blessings in disguise and so the queen could not hide her happiness and it spilt on her lips as smile. Her smile was actually the confirmation of her happiness and pride."

The queen who was present there said, "My Lord, Aushadha Kumar read my feelings perfectly well. The man's plight reminded me how fortunate I'm and I could not resist my smile." Aushadha

Kumar's analysis helped the king calm down. Since his anger vanished, he could judge in right way. He felt that the queen was innocent. "I'm sorry!" he said to the queen while taking her in his arm. The king thanked Aushadha Kumar for helping him to think justifiably. Once again, Pandit Dwivedi bit the dust and quietly tolerated the bitter taste of defeat. Aushadha Kumar's wisdom and prominence was no secret to the courtiers and a few courtiers' envy with Aushadha Kumar was not hidden from the king.

One day the king was sitting in the court with his courtiers. Suddenly he asked, "My wise courtiers, tell me who is superior – the person who is rich but fool or the person who is poor but intelligent?"

Pandit Dwivedi came forward first and said, "According to me the rich is always superior whether he is wise or fool."

"Why?" the king sought the reason.

"It's very simple, Huzoor! A man who is poor has to go to the rich to seek a job. However wise the person may be, the poor wise man has to work under a rich but stupid man. Then is it not clear, who is superior?" argued the Pandit.

The king heard him and then asked Aushadha Kumar, "What do you think about it?" Aushadha Kumar got up from his seat, bowed before the king and said, "Your Majesty, according to me, a wise poor man is far more superior than a fool rich man. If a man is rich but fool then he will not be able to take care of his wealth. If wealth is accumulated somewhere, it's the result of some wise persons' efforts and caution. A man may inherit riches, but will never be able to take care of it if he is a fool or if he does not get the assistance of a wise assistant. So a wise poor man is certainly better than a fool rich man."

Pandit Dwivedi fumed to hear such strong appealing argument. In his frustration he said to the king, "Your Majesty, Aushadha

Kumar is trying to trap us in his words' web. There is no need of such fictitious example to prove the point. It can be proved in more genuine way."

"Your majesty, your court is full of wise Pandits," Pandit Dwivedi appealed, "There is no dearth of supreme wisdom among your courtiers. Yet we work under you, bow before you, since you are rich and powerful. This is the clear and very evident example to prove my statement."

"But Your Majesty, our senior courtier fail to see the most prominent thing," Aushadha Kumar interrupted, "No doubt that we wise Pandits work for the king. However, the king can't work without the help of his wise counsellors. Is this not sufficient to prove who is superior than whom?"

Pandit Dwivedi had no words to refuse his laid argument and the king was extremely pleased with Pandit Aushadha. He got up from his seat, hugged him and praised aloud for his worthy courtier. The king was so happy that he gave Aushadha Kumar sixteen villages as his reward.

The queen loved Aushadha Kumar very much and considered him as his son. One day she called him in her chamber and asked, "Aushadha, it's prime time that you should marry a suitable girl. Should I find out a bride for you?"

Aushadha Kumar thanked the queen for her concern and replied, "O honourable queen, you are like my mother and I can understand your care and concern. But I would like to marry a girl of my choice."

The queen respected his wish and asked him to marry the girl whom he liked. After sometime, Aushadha Kumar found a bride for him. Her name was Aamra Devi. She was beautiful and very intelligent young woman from an ordinary family. Aushadha Kumar wedded Aamra Devi and visited the king and the queen to seek their blessings. The royal couple liked his choice and arranged a great feast to acknowledge the happy occasion. Pandit Dwivedi and other envious courtiers were further unhappy and disappointed with the growing prominence of Aushadha and his closeness with the royal couple. They began thinking a way out to lay Pandit Aushadha down in front of the king.

Then one day, Pundit Dwivedi found such an opportunity. After day's work when the king retired to his chamber, leaving his crown uncared in the assembly hall, Pandit Dwivedi quietly took out the precious gem tucked in the crown and placed in his pocket. Thereafter he hurried home. He took a pot full of curd, hid the gem inside and closed its mouth with a piece of cloth. He then called his maid handed over the pot and instructed, "Go to the lane where Aushadha Kumar and his wife live. Hawk there loudly to sale this curd. Remember sell this curd only when Aushadha Kumar's wife calls you."

Taking the pot, the maid set out to sale the curd. As per the instructions, she began hawking near Aushadha's house. A woman from neighbouring house called out, "What's the price of the curd?" But the maid didn't pay any heed. Aushadha Kumar's wife who was seeing it from the terrace was quite surprised by the woman's behaviour.

Meanwhile, another neighbouring woman heard the curd seller's call and asked the price. The maid again ignored the call and kept on hawking. Aushadha's wife felt it very odd. Next, she gave a call to the curd seller and she promptly responded and entered her house.

"What price do you want for your curd pot?" enquired the wife.

"It's my pleasure that you are taking curd from me. I don't want anything from great Pandit Aushadha Kumar's wife," saying so the maid got up and went away leaving the pot there.

The behaviour of the curd-selling woman aroused suspiscion in the mind of Aushadha Kumar's wife. She immediately called her maid and asked her to follow the strange woman secretly.

Meanwhile, in the palace the king found the gem of his crown missing. The king's men searched it everywhere but could not find it. The incident made the king unhappy and upset. Pandit Dwivedi and a few other envious courtiers came to meet the king. "Your Majesty, it must be the work of someone from us," said Pandit Dwivedi cunningly.

"Do you want to say I should suspect my own respectable courtiers?" asked the king quite surprised.

"There is nothing wrong in doing so, Your Majesty," said the Pandit, "After all a man's character can't be read from his face." Due to repeated insistence of his courtiers, the king decided to send his soldiers to search the houses of his courtiers.

In the meantime, the maid returned to Aushadha Kumar's wife and informed that the curd seller was none other than Pandit Dwivedi's maid. The wife was fully aware of Pandit Dwivedi's evil ways. But before the wife could inspect the curd to know the reason of such act, she heard the knock at her door. She opened the door to find the soldiers standing there with a search warrant.

The soldiers searched the house thoroughly and got the gem hidden in the curd pot. The soldiers returned with the recovered gem and informed the king where it was found. The king was furious to hear it. "Aushadha Kumar can do such nasty act. I can't believe it," the king murmured in his anger. Pandit Dwivedi and other envious Pandit fueled the king's anger.

Aushadha Kumar who had gone somewhere else returned home to get the bad news. His wife told him everything about Pandit Dwivedi's plot. Aushadha Kumar immediately rushed to the palace to meet the king. But the king was so much furious that he refused to meet him and sent a message to go away from there.

Aushadha Kumar was hurt. Since the king refused to listen to him, the next day he left the capital and set out for a remote village to live a secluded life. There he joined an old potter to work as his assistant. A few days passed. Pandit Dwivedi and fellow Pandits were happy that they could throw out their biggest hurdle. But the king soon began feeling the vacuum because of Aushadha Kumar's absence. The queen too was missing Aushadha Kumar. One day when the royal couple was talking to each other, the queen said, "I wish Aushadha Kumar should have been with us." The king said, "I miss him too. But his act was unpardonable."

"Maharaj," said the queen, "You must have heard him what he wanted to tell you. Everyone has right to prove his innocence and a king must hear him at least once." The king agreed to the queen. The next day he sent his soldiers in search of Aushadha

Kumar. After an exhaustive search, they found Aushadha in a village. They read the king's command. Aushadha Kumar accompanied the soldiers to the court. The king asked, "Aushadha, I want to listen to you regarding the recovered gem from your house."

"Your Majesty, I request you to allow me to bring my wife to the court who can explain it in better way." The king agreed. Aamra Devi appeared in the court with her maids and the curd's pot. "Your Majesty, the gem was found in this pot," said Aamra Devi showing the pot, "And it was brought to my place and was almost forced to keep it by a woman who came to sale it in our locality." "Who is she?" asked the king.

Aamra Devi indicated her maids to bring the woman in. The maids dragged a woman inside the court. It was the maid of Pandit Dwivedi. When Pandit Dwivedi saw his maid in the court, his face blanched.

"Who are you?" the king thundered.

"I'm Pandit Dwivedi's maid servant. Panditji told me to deliver the curd pot to Aushadha Kumar's house. It's none of my fault. Please forgive me," the woman begged. The king was raged to hear it. "You must get a severe punishment for hatching such conspiracy," said the king to Pandit Dwivedi. Pandit Dwivedi fell on the king's feet. "Please forgive me. I'll never do any such thing," begged the Pandit. "No you'll not get pardon from me. You are the culprit of Aushadha Kumar, only he can decide your fate. Pandit Aushadha kumar was a kind noble man. He didn't want to see anybody in trouble. So he requested the king to forgive him. The king was highly impressed by Aushadha's generosity. He asked the Pandit to beg forgiveness from Aushadha. Pandit Dwivedi did so in order to save himself. But in his heart he was even more revengeful. Aushadha Kumar's prestige enhanced greatly in the king's eyes. He made Aushadha Kumar the officer in charge of his military. Aushadha expressed his gratitude to the king, however Pandit Dwivedi was badly disappointed and frustrated with the promotion.

Pandit Dwivedi was not a person who mended his ways so easily. Soon he was up to his mischief. He pretended to be friendly with Aushadha. But in reality he was in search of some appropriate chance when he could distance away his rival from the king.

One day when Aushadha Kumar and Pandit Dwivedi were sitting together, Dwivedi said to Aushadha, "You are gem among the wisest. Please help me to understand the do's and don'ts of the life. Tell me, what a person should ensure first?"

"A person must understand the universal truth first," replied Pandit Aushadha.

"What is the next thing a person should secure?" asked Pandit Dwivedi.

"Wealth is the second most important thing a person should try to acquire," replied Pandit Aushadha.

"What is the third most important thing of our life?" asked Pandit Dwivedi.

"A person should learn 'Mantra' to work well," answered Aushadha.

"What is the next thing in which one should be accomplished?" asked Pandit Dwivedi.

"A person should then develop an ability to keep any secret within him," replied Pandit Aushadha.

"Can the secret be disclosed in front of any close one?" asked Pandit Dwivedi further.

"No not in front of anyone."

Pandit Dwivedi's cunning mind began thinking slyly. "I must take advantage of the sermon he gave in the end," thought Pandit Dwivedi. One day in an opportune moment, Pandit Dwivedi went to meet the king. The king was all alone. After some light talk, he said to the king, "Your Majesty, Pandit Aushadha is keeping some secret very close to him."

"Pandit!" said the king, "Refrain from thinking ills about Pandit Aushadha. Else you'll fall in trouble again."

"Believe me, Your Majesty!" said Pandit Dwivedi, "This time I'm not worried for my own welfare. I'm concerned for your well being which I guess is not so secure."

"What do you mean?" wondered the king.

"Your Majesty, I've come to know that Pandit Aushadha

is keeping some secret close to his heart."

"Pandit Dwivedi, what ever you are saying prove it," thundered the king.

"As you wish, Your Majesty," said Pundit Dwivedi, "Tomorrow in the court I'll prove it."

Next day when the king and other courtiers were present in the court, Pandit Dwivedi asked, "Pandit Aushadha Kumar do you ever divulge your secret to anyone?"

"No, not in front of anyone," replied Aushadha Kumar. "Don't you want to disclose your secrets in front of the king?"

Aushadha was a straightforward man. The principles he believed, he never budged from there and never hesitated to speak in front of anyone. So he said, "Yes, indeed I would not like to divulge the secret to anyone not even to the king."

The king's mind was already poisoned and so when he heard Pandit Aushadha Kumar, evil suspicion sprouted in his mind. Later on when the court was adjourned, he called Pandit Dwivedi and

discussed with him. "You Majesty, Please don't worry. I'll see that he should not carry out any of his evil plans," said the evil man.

After taking the king in his confidence, Pandit Dwivedi set out to meet his other friends. Meanwhile, Aushadha who saw the king worried and disturbed, well understood that it was none other than Pandit Dwivedi's cunning work. "I must follow him to get the information and to know about his plan," thought Aushadha. So Pandit Dwivedi reached the venue where he had called other four detractor Pandits to discuss the plan. The venue was a secluded grain godown. Following Pandit Dwivedi, Aushadha too entered the godown and hid himself behind stacks of grains. The other four Pandits also arrived. Pandit Dwivedi said, "It's an appropriate time when we should remove our enemy Pandit Aushadha Kumar from our path." "How can we do so?" asked the fellow courtiers.

"By killing him. That is the only way through which we can remove the hurdle from our path forever," replied Pandit Dwivedi. "What about the king? Will he not punish us for such gruesome crime?" asked the Pandits.

"No, he will not. I have already poisoned his mind and he is considering Aushadha as a danger who wants to topple him from his throne. In this case, the king will just welcome my move," replied Pandit Dwivedi.

Agreed to the plan they moved away from there. Pandit Aushadha Kumar also came out of his hideout. "I must take a quick decision and work fast, else I'll lose my life and a stigma will remain attached with my name even after my death," thought Aushadha. He immediately called urgent meeting of his loyal army officials and briefed them of his plan. Soon the army gathered around the palace and cordoned off from all the side. Army took total control over the palace and all the vital places. Pandit Aushadha was leading the army. When the king came to know about it, he was shocked. He felt that Pandit Dwivedi was absolutely right. After taking control over the capital and palace, Pandit Aushadha entered the palace to meet the king. He went near him and bowed before him. The king turned his face in anger. "Your Majesty," pleaded Pandit Aushadha, "You may be thinking that I'm a traitor who has come to arrest his king after taking administration in his own control. But this is not right. I'm still your loyal servant who can do anything for his king's wish."

The king was little surprised to hear him. He looke l at him with a doubt. "My Lord," said Aushadha Kumar, "How ɔan I do this to my beloved king who is no less than a father to me. Believe me, I'm forced to take such action just to bring a few truths in front of you. I didn't have much time to wait and convince you, since my life was in danger."

Pandit Aushadha told everything to the king. All the suspicion and doubts were washed away from the king's mind. He got up from his seat and hugged Aushadha Kumar. The king summoned Pandit Dwivedi and other four Pandits. They were aghast to see that their plan failed badly. Pandit Aushadha said, "Pandit Dwivedi, you must be wondering how I came to know about your conspiracy? Do you remember once I told you that a secret must not be opened in front of anyone? But it seems it didn't appeal to you and you shared your conspiracy plan with your friend's and then I too benefited from your revelation."

Pandit Dwivedi and his associates had no place to hide their faces. The king said angrily, "Pandit Dwivedi, many times in the past you tried to vilify my mind. But this time you crossed all the limits. You must be punished severely. You all are dismissed from your respectable jobs and being ordered to work as slaves of Aushadha Kumar."

However, Aushadha Kumar was no ordinary soul. He pleaded

the king, "Your Majesty, though they are defaulters, all their faults are the product of their selfish attitude. They took shelter to evil ways because they failed to admire other person's ability. But despite all, I would not like to use them as my slaves. Since they are learned people, I request you to free them from slavery." The Pandit's fell on Aushadha Kumar's feet in gratefulness. On Pandit Aushadha Kumar's request, Pandit Dwivedi and other Pandits were freed from slavery.

Pandit Aushadha Kumar led an illustrious life. It is said that he was no ordinary soul but reincarnation of 'Bodhisatva'.

The Jackal & Mantra

Pandit Ramchandra Shastri was the royal priest of the kingdom of Varanasi. King Surendra Singh, the king of Varanasi had great respect for the royal priest. The royal priest well deserved such honour. He was a great scholar, a pious person and gave top most importance to the well being of his kingdom.

Once a calamity befell on the kingdom of Varanasi. One year it did not rain and the kingdom faced severe famine. The poor began dying of hunger. There was hue and cry everywhere. The king put all his means to salvage his people but the situation remained out of control. The anxious king met the royal priest and discussed the worrying situation. King Surendra Singh requested

the priest to find a solution out of the crisis. The royal priest was his last hope. Pandit Ramchandra Shastri too was sad for the plight of the people. He said to the king, "O king, only rain can save our people and kingdom. I know an eternal mantra known as Brahma Mantra. The powerful mantra has capacity to please God Indra and bring the rain. For the cause of our people, I'll go to the deep forest and practice the mantra for some time."

The king heaved a sigh of relief and thanked the priest. Next day, Panditji went to the deep forest and in a secluded place, he sat with closed eyes and began chanting mantra. A jackal who was passing by the place, heard the chanting. The sight made him curious and he sat at some distance. The jackal knew that the man in front of him was no ordinary man but a scholar. He had some idea that knowledge could make a person superior from others. So he thought, "If I learn the mantra I too can be superior than the other animals of the forest and in due course become the king of the forest."

Enthused by the thought, the jackal began listening to the mantras and chanting in his mind in order to learn them. A long practice of mantra pleased the Rain God and it began raining in the region. Panditji's penance was complete. He opened his eyes with happiness but was shocked to find a jackal sitting in front of him and repeating the mantra.

Panditji's eyes met with the jackal. The jackal smiled a sly smile and said, "Panditji, I learnt your magic mantra. Now I'm as great and powerful as you. I too am a scholar like you. Ha, Ha, Ha!" The royal priest was badly perturbed to hear him and his cunning laughter. "Brahma mantra is indeed very powerful. But it has fallen in a wrong hand. If this stupid uses, it will cause blunder," thought the priest anxiously. I must catch him and kill him, the root of all the trouble in future."

Thinking so, the royal priest ran to catch the jackal. However, the jackal was careful. He ran with great speed. There cannot be any match between a human being and a wild animal when it comes to running in the forest. So the agile jackal vanished in forest leaving the priest tired and worried. The royal priest returned to the kingdom. The rain soon established normal life in the kingdom.

Meanwhile, the learned jackal was very proud of his newly acquired status. He considered himself a single great scholar among all the animals of the jungle and began thinking to capture the king's throne. "I must marry before ascend the throne," thought the jackal.

The jackal then went to meet the king of the jackals. He apprised him of his freshly acquired position and expressed his wish to marry his daughter. King Jackal liked the scholar jackal and agreed to give his daughter in marriage. After marriage the jackal became the son-in-law of the king.

Soon the news of the learned jackal reached all the small and big animals of the jungle. Initially, the small animals came to see the jackal. They heard him chanting mantra and were impressed. They touched his feet in reverence and went away. The animals who returned after meeting the learned jackal informed their other friends. Soon jungle folks like fox, wolf, monkeys, bears, elephants and leopard all were queuing up in front of the learned jackal's house to hear him chanting mantra and to get his blessings.

The learned jackal had become such a power that King Lion decided to visit him and accept his supremacy. So one day, King Lion went to meet the learned jackal and paid his respect to him. Since the king of the jungle, lion too accepted the supremacy of

him. The jackal became the new king of the jungle. However, all the power and honour virtually turned his head. He began thinking to capture the throne of Varanasi. So one day, he addressed all the jungle folks including the previous king, lion, "Dear friends, as your know I'm armed with power like Brahma mantra. Now we are no less intelligent than human beings are. Wisdom was the only faculty where we were behind the human beings. Now with this newly acquired position, we are in no way less capable than our enemies are. Our physical strength is matchless. So we must attack on Varanasi and capture the city for us."

The audience agreed to the jackal and applauded him for his plan. So to work on the proposal, the next day all the animals gathered at one place, made a big procession and began moving towards Varanasi. The procession was led by the new king, jackal. He was sitting on a lion who was standing on the two elephants.

The odd attackers reached the gate of the Varanasi city. There King Jackal sent his messenger, Wolf to the king of Varanasi with a challenge to fight with them. When the Varanasi King heard the message, he was puzzled as well as scared. He called the royal priest immediately and informed him about the threat. The king was unable to believe that the wild animals who were generally scared of the human beings had come to fight with them. He asked the priest, "How come these animals be so intelligent and brave? There must be some reason."

The royal priest remembered the jackal who learnt his mantra. He immediately understood the whole matter.

Meanwhile, the people heard about the attack and hid themselves in their houses. The wild attackers were finding it difficult to wait so they entered the city and reached near the king's palace. Everyone was scared including the king. The king was unable to understand how to deal with their wildness.

But the royal priest was calm. He had full faith on his wisdom. "An animal's intelligence cannot supersede a human's wisdom," he said to himself. The priest stood on the palace's terrace and addressed King Jackal, "Why have you come here?" The jackal replied, "Didn't you get our message that we've come to fight with you? Can't you see my big brave army?"

"Is this your army Honourable King Jackal? Your army includes a diverse kind of animals. You are the leader of an army, which has much bigger and brave animals than its leader. I doubt that the lion will comply with your order," remarked the priest shrewdly.

The jackal didn't like the remark. He felt insulted and said, "O priest, how dare you doubt my credibility. If my followers will not listen to me then whom will they listen to?"

"Don't be angry King Jackal," said the priest, "I just expressed my apprehension. I doubt that these lions will obey your order.

Why don't you check it before attacking on us?"

The doubt angered the jackal further. To show the priest how the lion obeyed him, he said to the lion, "O brave lion, roar as loud as you can." The lion complied with the command and roared so loudly that the sky began resounding with his uproar. The elephants on which the lion was standing, thought that the lion was going to kill them. So they began running helter-skelter. The lion who was standing on the elephants fell down and King Jackal too followed him to the ground. Then began a grea amount of confusion among the gathered animals and they began running haphazardly. The small animals were being trampled under the elephant's feet. There were cries and fear among the animal's army. They all rushed away from the palace and towards the jungle. The royal priest's wisdom worked. He immediately asked the guards to catch the fraud jackal and kill him. The jackal was soon caught and killed by the guards. The other animals ran away to the forest to save their lives.

Varanasi King who witnessed everything with his own eyes came to the royal priest and hugged him. The king said, "Till a wise person like you remains in Varanasi, our kingdom will be always safe from the trouble."

The True Devotee

In ancient India there was a small remote village named Narayanpur. There lived a poor landless labour named 'Ghisa'. One morning when Ghisa came out of the house in search of work and walked through the village lanes, he saw the Village Head sitting in Panchayat Office and talking to a village crowd who had gathered in front of the office. The Village Head was calling the persons turn by turn and was asking a similar question, "Yes, how many people should I write in front of your name?"

One by one, they came to the Head and asked to write five, two, seven, six, ten, twenty.... Ghisa was puzzled to see the whole sight. "Why the people are gathered here and about what are they writing this number?" Ghisa wondered.

Suddenly, the Head's eyes fell on Ghisa. He called him and said, "Yes, Ghisa! Should I write your name also in the list? Tell me, how many people should I write on front of your name?" Ghisa was still not clear which number the Head was talking about. So he asked, "What kind of list you are making, Sir? I am not aware of anything." The Head replied, "Ghisa, in which world are you living? Don't you know that tomorrow Swami Kashyapji, the great pupil of Lord Buddha is paying his visit with one thousand Boddh monks? Since it's not possible to feed the great number of monks at one place or in any one house, the villagers have decided to feed the monks at their respective places. Each one is taking the responsibility of a few monks depending upon their capacity. Now tell me how many monks will you feed?"

Ghisa was a poor man. Very hesitantly he replied, "Sir, you know my wretched condition. It's difficult for me to feed my family everyday. How can I invite any guest at home?"

The Village Head said, "You are indeed a poor man but today you made yourself poorest by denying a golden opportunity to feed a guest. A guest is form of the God and everyday we don't get such chance."

The words of Village Head pierced like arrow in the heart of Ghisa. He said, "Sir, you are absolutely right. I will ma age and certainly feed the guest. Please write 'one monk' in front of my name."

Meanwhile, the village moneylender appeared there. He was a rich man. He said loudly to Village Head, "Sir, write one hundred guests in front of my name!" The man ensured that everyone around should hear it. Ghisa too heard it and felt himself poorer than before. "Where one hundred guest and where just one guest!

There is no comparison between the two," he thought sadly walking away from there. But for Ghisa feeding one guest too was a big thing. He knew that there was nothing at home and he would have to arrange all by tomorrow lunch. Plunged in thought, he reached the home and informed his wife about the guest. The wife became very happy to hear it. She said, "It's very nice that tomorrow a guest is visiting our house. We will labour hard and earn good enough to feed our guest well. What if we are poor! We will not let this feel to the guest monks." The happiness and enthusiasm in the wife's words relieved Ghisa. With rejuvenated will to serve their guest, the couple set out of the house in search of work. When Ghisa and his wife were passing by the moneylender's house, he was called out, "Ghisa!" It was moneylender. Ghisa went near him. He said, "Ghisa, you know that tomorrow a big number of Buddha monks are visiting my house on lunch. A big amount of dry firewood is required to prepare food for them. Will you cut the wood by evening? You'll be paid handsomely. But remember you must finish your work by the evening."

Ghisa threw a gaze on the heap of wood logs. It was a big heap. "Probably it'll be difficult to finish the work by the evening," thought Ghisa. "But I must accept it. If I finish the work, I will be able to feed my guest well. Ghisa nodded for the work. He thanked the God for providing work for him so soon. He sent his wife home to look after the household chores. Ghisa with full of determination began his work. He worked continuous for hours. He knew that if he sat to rest he would not be able to finish his work and then would not get his remuneration. Till evening his whole body was tired and aching. His hands had developed numerous sores. But Ghisa was not bothered for all the pains. He has single mission in his mind. He wanted to get good return for his work so that he could feed his guest well and for that he had to finish

his work by the evening. When darkness began spreading Ghisa finished with his work. The moneylender was really happy to see him work so hard. "I was not confident that you'll be able to finish the work today. You've alone done the work of ten men. I am very happy," said the moneylender.

The moneylender then called his servant and briefed him. The servant returned with a bag basketful of rice, a basketful of pulse and a basketful of many green vegetables. The moneylender said, "Ghisa, accept all these things as your remuneration. Tomorrow you too have to serve a guest. Now go home without any worry."

Ghisa was startled to see so much rice, pulse and vegetables. Never before, he got such compensation for his work. Ghisa thanked the God in his heart, accepted everything and returned home happily. When the wife saw him with so many things, she became very happy. All the worries of the couple vanished. They planned to give their guest a good feast so that he should not feel less cared and served than the guests of rich villagers.

Next morning the couple woke up and became busy to clean their small house. Suddenly Ghisa heard a stranger's call from outside. He came out of the house and saw a man standing out on the entrances. "I am a cook," the stranger introduced himself with folded hands, "I've come to know that today a special guest is visiting your house. I've come here in a hope to get a work here."

"I am sorry, friend! We are poor people we can't hire a cook for the purpose. My wife and I'll manage the household work," said Ghisa to the man.

"If you are so much poor then I'll not seek any payment for the work. But I would like to serve the guest by cooking the food for him and in such pious work you too can't stop me," saying so the stranger entered the house and began helping his wife in the kitchen. Ghisa was very much surprised but he could not stop him from doing so. After managing the things at home, Ghisa set out for Village Head's house to bring his guest. When he reached near the house, it gave a deserted look. Ghisa met the Village Head and said, "Sir, I've come to take my guest. Please oblige me by sending him with me."

Village Head checked his notebook to see the name of the guest written in front of Ghisa's name. But he found the name missing from the notebook. By mistake, he had forgot to include Ghisa's name in the notebook. "I am very sorry Ghisa," Village Head expressed his regret, "All guest monks have been sent with their respective hosts. Now there is no guest left whom I can send with you."

Ghisa was badly disappointed to hear such news. He felt as if a big misfortune befell on him. The couple had worked hard with full dedication and will, to serve their guest. But the opportunity was snatched by the destiny. Ghisa cried in his heart, "How will I go home and inform this to my wife who must be anxiously waiting to welcome the guest monk?"

Ghisa walked towards home thinking gloomily. "I can't go home alone like this," he thought. On the way, he saw a Boddh monk sitting under a tree and preaching a big crowd in front of him. Ghisa's eyes twinkled to see him. He rushed near him prostrated in front of him and began crying. The monk consoled Ghisa and asked the reason of his grief. Ghisa said, "Your Holiness only you can help me out of my grief. My wife and I will be greatly pleased if you visit my house for lunch today. If you didn't do so, we will surely die out of grief."

Ghisa was indeed crying like a child. The monk smiled and said, "That is the reason my child! Don't cry. I am ready to accompany you." The very moment the monk got up from his seat, leaving his audience startled to see him going with a poor ordinary villager. He walked with Ghisa towards his hut. Ghisa was jubilant. He felt as if he got the whole world's wealth."

Leaving the audience in surprise the monk walked but the people were unable to believe their own eyes. Ghisa might be ignorant about the identity of the monk but the people of the gathering knew that he was none other than Swami Sthavir, the greatest pupil of Lord Buddha. Swami Sthavir was considered another form of Lord Buddha. The news of Swamiji's visit to Ghisa's place for lunch, spread like wild fire in the village. It was indeed the matter of great amazement for the villagers that

the man, who refused to have lunch at Village Head's house, obliged Ghisa for the same. Village Head and the other villagers gathered near Ghisa's hut. They saw Ghisa and his wife washing Swamiji's feet with devotion and then serving lunch to their guest with great respect and care. They observed cook in Ghisa's house with surprise and they were astonished to see Swamiji enjoying the food with great relish.

Swamiji finished his lunch. Ghisa and his wife were greatly satisfied. They said, "O Lord, by accepting my invitation, you've honoured a poor man like me."

Swamiji said, "Ghisa no one in this world is poor or rich. In the God's eyes, each of his creation is equal. Work is the real worship of God. The God has acknowledged your hard work, your dedication and your services. The people of the world might have ignored it but not the God. Your cook...."

"But Lord, it's not my cook," interrupted Ghisa, "I am a poor man I can't hire a cook. This man was stranger to me till morning when he came here and pestered me to accept his services for such pious cause."

Hardly Ghisa had completed his sentence when the people marked the cook flying in the air towards sky. People held their breath.

Suddenly a voice came from the sky and resounded, "Ghisa, you are a true devotee of the God. I'm God Indra. I had come to test your devotion. I observed your hard work. You fed Lord Buddha with love, dedication and devotion. He is greatly pleased. However, he is very much sad with your poverty and so I'm freeing you from all your misery."

The people saw the sight with wide eyes and heard the words from Heaven in disbelief. "The cook was no other than Lord Indra," people whispered to each other in amazement.

Suddenly the sky was overcast with gray clouds just above

the small hut of Ghisa and from these clouds the gold coins, precious jewels and stones began raining in Ghisa's house.

"It's all for you Ghisa!" the voice from Heaven said, "It's the reward from Lord Buddha in return of your labour and dedication." Ghisa and his wife were overwhelmed to see the lord's love for him."

Ghisa was poor and belonged to low caste, so the villagers had always treated him shabbily. However, the people standing around regretted for their past hatred towards him. Everything changed in a moment. Bathing in God's grace Ghisa and his wife were looking much more honourable than any other member of the village. Village Head came forward and hugged Ghisa with love. He said, "with the grace of Swamiji you are now the richest man of not only village but of the whole kingdom. You are the real devotee of the God!" Ghisa fell on Swamiji Sthavir's feet. Swamiji blessed Ghisa and went away, leaving him feeling grateful to the God's amazing love and care.

✳ ✳ ✳

The Magic of Enterprise

Long long ago, in the city of Varanasi there lived a young, unemployed and poor youth whose name was Mohan. One day he was wandering in a city road in search of a suitable job. At some distance from him, the chief treasurer of the kingdom was passing with his friend. "Under your governance and skill the treasury is full of riches. The king admires you and you are one of the closest man of the king," said the friend to the treasurer, "I often wonder what are the qualities which make you so special?"

The treasurer smiled and said, "Nothing big my friend! It's just the magic of intelligent hard work." The treasurer stopped for a while and looked around. He saw a dead mouse lying at some distance. He pointed towards it and said, "An enterprising man can earn even from that dead mouse and initiate his own small business." The words amused the friend. The treasurer and his friend passed from there talking to each other. But if left a deep impression on the young man who was overhearing their conversation. He went near the dead mouse and picked it up with his fingers. "What can I do with this?" Mohan asked himself, "But the treasurer is an able and experienced man."

Swinging between his positive and negative thoughts, the

young man moved ahead holding the mouse in his hand. "Will you sell your mouse?" The young man was interrupted from his thoughts by a passerby, "I want it for my cat." The man was holding his pet in his arm. "Mouse!" the young man whispered waking up from his thoughts. "Yes, of course!" replied Mohan gleefully. The owner of the cat placed one paisa coin on his palm in return for the dead mouse and went away from there. Mohan was still unable to believe that he had made his first earning of his life from the dead mouse. The words of the treasurer resounded in his ears, "Initiative, enterprise and hard labour can take any one to great height!" Clinching the shining one-paisa coin in his fist, Mohan stepped ahead with a new hope and sure mantra of success.

He went to the grocery shop and bought jaggery worth one paisa. Mohan then filled a big pot with water and taking jaggery and water; he walked to edge of the forest. Mohan was well aware that there was no drinking water available at that secluded place and if he could provide it to the passerby there, that would be a great relief for them. So he sat on the lane, which led to the forest witht the water and jaggery. As the sun set, the flower pickers who had gone to the forest to collect the flowers, began returning with the basket of flowers over their head. They were tired and thirsty after a long day's work. Mohan who was waiting for this moment called out, "Brothers, you look tired and thirsty. Please take some water and jaggery." The relief, which the labourers felt to hear this, was no less than finding an oasis in desert. They all rushed to him. Mahon gave each one a piece of jaggery and quenched their thirst with the water.

The flower pickers were really happy and grateful to Mohan. As a mark of their gratitude, they generously gave him flowers from their baskets in return for his services. The labourers went on their way and after a while Mohan too returned to the city with a basketful of fresh and fragrant flowers. Mohan visited the city temple. The people were gathering there for the evening prayer. In no time, his flowers were bought by the devotees. Mohan was indeed surprised to see ten copper coins in his hand at the end of the day. "It is the power of enterprise and hard work which provided me ten coins, beginning from nothing," whispered Mohan. He returned home content and with a new enthusiasm. Next day he bought more jaggery with a part of his earning and visited the forest with more jaggery and a bigger pot of water. He at there for longer hours than previous day, served more people than the earlier day and of course got more flowers to sell.

After quenching their thirst, Mohan moved towards the nearby village. A group of grass cutters was working under the blazing sun. He went near them and asked politely, "Would you like to have some water with jaggery?"

"Yes of course!" said all of them in chorus. Mohan helped them to drink water with his striking humbleness. The field workers were extremely pleased and thankful to his selfless services. Everyday Mohan visited the fields with remaining water and jaggery after paying his visit to the forest path.

The services provided to the flower pickers gave him bundles of flowers in return and helped him to earn mone, whereas serving the field workers gave him numerous friends who could do anything for him if it's required. It went like this for a month.

One day Mohan was passing by the royal garden, which was full of trees and flowers. Suddenly a storm erupted. The furious cyclone threw everything in complete chaos. The trees were uprooted, branches of almost all trees succumbed to the storm's fury and fell on the ground. When the storm calmed down, the royal garden was filled with broken branches, leaves and uprooted trees.

The beautiful garden had taken an ugly face. The royal

gardener was horrified to see the destruction. Mohan, who had taken shelter somewhere nearby, saw the branches and leaves littered all over the garden. Mohan's enterprising mind began thinking. He went near the old royal gardener and said politely, "Sir, you look anxious. Can I be of any help?"

"Help! How can you help me young man?" said the gardener in a worried tone, "I'm badly in trouble. The king is suposed to be here at any moment. If he sees all this mess, I'll certainly lose my job."

"I can clean it if you allow me to keep the trees, branches and leaves," said the young man.

"I can allow you to do so happily, only if you do so fast," replied the gardener promptly. "Sure, Sir," said Mohan and rushed out. He saw a few urchins playing on the road. He went near them and said lovingly, "Dear children, I've brought sweet jaggery for you." Hearing this all of them mobbed around him spreading their palms for a piece of jaggery. Mohan obliged each one of them with a small piece and then said, "I can give you more of it, if you help me a little." The Little children had all greed for the sweet. They readily agreed to help.

"What should I do for you?" asked the children. "Nothing much! Just help me to clean the royal garden," said Mohan. The children rushed to the royal garden with Mohan and with their joint effort cleaned the garden in a very little time. The royal gardener was indeed happy with Mohan's efficient work. He allowed him to take the trees, branches and leaves with him. As Mohan had promissed, he provided the children generously with jaggery. Children were happy to get the sweet jaggery and went back to their playing. Mohan was even happier.

He cut trees into pieces and with al the woods, twigs and leaves sat on the way to sell them. After sometime, a potter passed by the way in his cart. Seeing the wood and twigs he came near and asked, "Would you like to sell these? I need it for my pots."

"Yes, it's for sale, Sir," said Mohan. The potter gave him twenty copper coins in return. Mohan helped him to load the twigs and leaves on his cart. The potter asked before leaving, "I'm going to the market. If you've to go somewhere in the city, you can come with me." Mohan's way to home passed through the market. So he sat with him on the cart. When they reached the market, Mohan saw a few people standing at one place. One of them said, "Do you know, tomorrow it will be the crowded and busy day of the market. Horse traders from different parts of the country are visiting Varanasi city."

Their conversation was overheard by Mohan. His enterprising mind began thinking fast. "I must not let this opportunity go," he said to himself and rushed to his village friends. Mohan met them

and said, "Friends, I need your help."

"We'll be happy to help you. Please tell what do you want from us," replied the grass cutters in chorus. "Will each one of you give me a bundle of grass?" asked Mohan. "Hey, this is just a small thing which you are asking from your friends," said the grass cutters, "We are total five hundred workers and so five hundred bundles of grass will be kept aside for you." Mohan thanked for their gesture and said further, "Friends, I want one more favour from you. Until tomorrow evening, you do not sale your grass to anyone. Not a single buyer should get grass from you." "We'll do it for you," promised the grass cutters. As it was decided, the grass cutters stacked the five hundred grass bundles at one place. Mohan came in the evening and transported those to the market.

Next day early in the morning, the horse traders began pouring in Varanasi city. However, despite all information about horse fair, the grass was totally absent from the market. The traders were puzzled. They wandered in the market in search of grass and then at one place they found bundles of green grass stack·d. They all rushed there. No one else other than Mohan was the owner of the grass bundles. Due to less supply and big demand, the humble grass had become a precious thing. The traders wer· ready to pay the price much higher than the price on usual days. Mohan did a good business. He earned two thousand copper coins from them. Mohan was very happy. His humble behaviour and hard work in past had paid him with handsome dividends.

A few days later Mohan went to the market. He found most of the shops closed and market less crowded than the other days. Unable to see the clear reason for such quietness, Mohan enquired with one of the shopkeepers. The shopkeeper informed, "Tomorrow a merchant from distant land is arriving through water way. He is bringing his goods in boats. All the traders from our city are busy in the preparation for his visit. Tomorrow all of them will go to buy goods from him. That's why the market is giving a deserted look."

Mohan's eyes sparkled to hear the news and mind began thinking fast. As soon as he got an idea, he started working in that direction. Firstly, he bought a fine dress for himself and then hired an elegant carriage pulled by handsome horses. Next day as the dawn broke, he wore new dress, rode the carriage with two of his friends and reached the bank of the river where the merchandise was supposed to arrive. A little later Mohan saw the boats coming towards the bank. He briefed his friends and readied himself to welcome the merchant. When the boats touched the bank, Mohan was the first and only person to be present there. "Welcome to our city," said Mohan warmly. He introduced himself as city's trader. After a few introductory exchanges, he expressed his wish to buy all the goods from him. The merchant from other land put a price for his goods, which Mohan agreet to pay happily.

"I may take a few days' time to arrange for such a big money," said Mohan, "However, as a security for our deal, please accept my gold ring." Mohan slipped out the ring and placed on merchant's palm. The merchant had no problem in waiting for a few days, after all he was promised to get the handsome return for his goods. After agreeing on such deal, Mohan returned to his friends and at some distance from the bank pitched a tent. Clean mattresses were placed on the floor and a number of cushions and pillows were placed. Mohan sat there elegantly enjoying the comfort and softness of cushion. He asked one of his friends to stand outside the tent and bring in the traders of the city resectfully who he guessed would soon be approaching him.

In the meanwhile, after sometime, the traders of the city began pouring in on the bank. All of them wanted to buy goods. The market of Varanasi heavily depended on those imported goods and traders would wait for the arrival patiently. So such occasion was very very important for them. However, when they met the merchant from foreign land, they were informed that all the goods were sold off. Imagine the amount of shock and disappointment perceived by the traders of Varanasi! "How can that happen and who bought all the goods?" was their spontaneous query.

"The man is presently taking shelter in that tent," the merchant pointed towards Mohan's tent. The traders were bewildered. "Who could be this man?" they discussed with each other as they moved away from there, "The man obviously does not belong to our group."

"Whoever he may be, but he has bought all the goods. We are certainly ruined," said one of the traders.

"We must not let that happen in any case. After all it's the question of our survival," said the other man anxiously.

"But what can we do now?" questioned another disappointed voice.

"We must buy all the merchandise from this outsider to keep him away from the fray. We'll offer him to pay a much higher price for goods and obviously he would not refuse" said one of the traders. The solution appealed to all of them. So after making their plan, they all went near Mohan's camp and expressed their wish to meet Mohan. The friend who was standing outside the tent took them inside. Mohan offered seats to all of them and with a pleasant smile asked the reason for their visit. "We want to buy a part of your goods, which you have bought from the merchant," said the traders in chorus. "But I have bought it to start my own business," said Mohan showing a little unwillingness to sell off the goods. "We can pay you handsomely," said the trader in desperate voice, "We can pay you more than what you will be actually able to earn from it." After a little refusal, Mohan agreed to sell off the goods in much higher price than he was going to pay for it to the merchant. The traders were happy with the deal thought it cost them heavily. They had satisfaction that they could succeed in keeping an outsider away from their business. As per the deal, all the them immediately paid off the money. With less than half of the money received, Mohan paid off the merchant for his goods. The remaining one lakh gold coins he profited with his wisdom and virtually with no capital.

In just a few months, he had become a rich man. Mohan remembered the words of the treasurer. "It's all because of the wise words of our respected treasurer. He is my mentor and I must offer Gurudakshina to him," said Mohan to himself. After arriving at such conclusion, he parted half of his earning, placed it in a bag and went to the treasurer's house. When Mohan met the treasurer, he touched his feet and offered the bag. "It's my Gurudakshina, Sir. Please accept it. I've earned all these due to your advice." "My advice? Gurudakshina? What are you saying man?" said the treasurer in a puzzled tone, "Do you think we have ever met before?"

Mohan told him everything starting from the dead mouse and his remarks, which he had overheard. He narrated the whole story of his success. The treasurer was startled to hear his tale. "It's amazing! The boy is extremely intelligent, hard working, enterprising and dedicated to his work. He'll certainly be very successful in his life and acquire a big position. This boy matches with my dream groom for my only daughter," thought the treasurer. The treasurer got up from his seat and hugged him warmly. The treasurer introduced him to his wife and daughter. The wife too liked Mohan very much. The treasurer couple purposed to give their daughter's hand to him. For Mohan, no other surprise could be bigger and prettier than to get a lovely bride and to become the son-in-law of such a respectable man. He jubilantly nodded. Soon the young couple was married with pomp and show. Mohan led a happy, comfortable and very successful life with his wife, children and of course in the guardianship of his guru, the treasurer.

✳ ✳ ✳

The End